"Let me see you to your car."

She flicked her eyes back to his, her expression carrying a hint of question but not the suspicion that had been there earlier. "That's not necessary."

"Yes, it is. I need to know you're safe. I couldn't live with myself if I just walked away and something happened to you."

She raised her chin as if she'd figured him out. "Because I'm the new boss's sister and an executive at Kendall?"

"No. I suppose that's a good reason, but it's not my primary one." Of course, technically protecting the boss's sister *was* his reason for being there, but the words felt good on his tongue.

She tilted her head to the side and arched her eyebrows as if waiting for him to come clean.

"Let's just say I'll be thinking about you all night. I don't want those thoughts to be laced with worry." It sounded like a line, and as soon as he'd said it he'd wanted it back. The ironic thing was, it was one of the first honest things he'd said to her.

ANN VOSS PETERSON

SECRET PROTECTOR

TORONTO NEW YORK LONDON
AMSTERDAM PARIS SYDNEY HAMBURG
STOCKHOLM ATHENS TOKYO MILAN MADRID
PRAGUE WARSAW BUDAPEST AUCKLAND

To those who put others before themselves.
The definition of a hero.

Special thanks and acknowledgment to Ann Voss Peterson for her contribution to the Situation: Christmas series.

PLEASE RECYCLE
THIS PRODUCT IS RECYCLABLE

ISBN-13: 978-0-373-74633-0

Recycling programs
for this product may
not exist in your area.

SECRET PROTECTOR

www.Harlequin.com

Printed in U.S.A.

ABOUT THE AUTHOR

Ever since she was a little girl making her own books out of construction paper, Ann Voss Peterson wanted to write. So when it came time to choose a major at the University of Wisconsin, creative writing was her only choice. Of course, writing wasn't a *practical* choice—one needs to earn a living. So Ann found jobs, including proofreading legal transcripts, working with quarter horses and washing windows. But no matter how she earned her paycheck, she continued to write the type of stories that captured her heart and imagination: romantic suspense. Ann lives near Madison, Wisconsin, with her husband, her two young sons, her border collie and her quarter horse mare. Ann loves to hear from readers. Email her at ann@annvosspeterson.com or visit her website at www.annvosspeterson.com.

Books by Ann Voss Peterson

HARLEQUIN INTRIGUE
745—THE BOYS IN BLUE
    "LIAM"
780—LEGALLY BINDING
838—DESERT SONS
    "TOM"
878—MARITAL PRIVILEGE
925—SERIAL BRIDE*
931—EVIDENCE OF MARRIAGE*
937—VOW TO PROTECT*
952—CRITICAL EXPOSURE
981—SPECIAL ASSIGNMENT
1049—WYOMING MANHUNT
1095—CHRISTMAS AWAKENING
1133—PRICELESS NEWBORN PRINCE
1160—COVERT COOTCHIE-COOTCHIE-COO
1202—ROCKY MOUNTAIN FUGITIVE
1220—A RANCHER'S BRAND OF JUSTICE
1238—A COP IN HER STOCKING
1257—SEIZED BY THE SHEIK
1312—SECRET PROTECTOR

*Wedding Mission

CAST OF CHARACTERS

Grayson Scott—In his wildest dreams, the former navy SEAL turned bodyguard never imagined he'd fall in love with the woman he was hired to protect. And in his darkest nightmares, he never conceived he was the one putting her in danger.

Natalie Kendall—A romantic at heart, Natalie spent her life searching for a man she could count on. Little did she know, she had to learn to count on herself before she was ready for the love she craved.

The stranger at the coffee shop—He was the reason Gray and Natalie met. Was he also part of the threat that faced them?

Devon, Ash and Thad Kendall—Natalie's big brothers want to protect her from life. Too bad that's not possible.

Jimbo Russel—Gray's friend and member of his Navy SEAL team, Jimbo was killed on a mission in Yemen. Gray will always blame himself for his buddy's death.

Sherry Russel—Gray's best friend's wife will never forgive him for her husband's death.

Maxim Miles—The art dealer believes he's entitled to a piece of Natalie's talent. How far will he go to collect?

Demetrius Jones—Natalie's ex-boyfriend was always after her money and connections. Now that they aren't together, nothing has changed.

Chapter One

If Natalie didn't need an infusion of caffeine so badly she could barely see straight, she'd walk out of the coffee shop right now, despite already having paid for her latte.

She checked her watch and tried to resist the urge to tap the toe of her pump on the tile floor. She could feel the man next to her give her a once-over. Dressed in jeans, with shirttails hanging out and shoes that looked more like slippers than street wear, he was probably thinking she was uptight.

He was probably right.

Six foot, thin build, he was also kind of cute, at least in an ordinary sort of way.

What the heck? She was usually drawn to the good-looking ones. Maybe it was past time to shake things up. Taking a deep breath and curving her lips into a smile, she gave him a glance.

He looked away.

Figures. Natalie's luck with men was right up there with her talent for finding short lines.

She peered at the darkness outside the coffee shop's glass doors. Jolie would be finished trying on bridesmaids' dresses before Natalie even reached the bridal shop. And Rachel would surely be finished with the fitting for her wedding dress. Natalie wouldn't even get a glimpse. She was on schedule to let down both her future sisters-in-law and disappoint herself, and for what?

Caffeine was a horrible addiction.

"Double shot, low-fat latte?" The barista raised a pierced brow and plunked the cup on the counter.

Natalie flashed her best imitation of a grateful smile, picked up the coffee. She dodged her fellow addicts and pushed out the door, chimes jingling in her ear.

A chill wind hit her face. November in St. Louis was unpredictable, but one bit of weather that she could count on was that winter would eventually arrive. Apparently it had sometime in the past half hour. Using her free hand to wrap her trench more tightly around her, she made a mental note to dig out her wool coat before work tomorrow.

Her heels clacked hollow on the sidewalk.

Dark windows stared down at her from all angles. City noises drifted on the breeze, sounding as if they were coming from the riverfront, blocks away. The temperature wasn't the only thing to have changed in the time she'd been stuck in the coffee shop. Since she'd last walked the three blocks from the office, the business district seemed to have vacated for the night.

The bell on the coffee shop's door jingled, as someone followed her into the cold.

She crossed the side street midblock and headed back toward Kendall Communications and the executive parking garage. The drive to the bridal shop wouldn't take long. And Jolie would try her dress on again, if need be. The night was looking up.

The sound of footsteps shuffled behind her.

She glanced back. The silhouette of a man strode along the sidewalk. Tall, thin, shirt-tails flapping in the breeze. Must be the guy from the coffee shop, although on second glance, his hands were empty. Shouldn't he be carrying a cup?

She quickened her pace.

She was being silly. She knew it. But there was something about the dark and the quiet and the cold that set her nerves on edge.

She just needed to get to the Kendall building. There she could duck into the parking garage and the guy behind her would continue down the sidewalk to wherever it was he was headed.

She turned the corner, half expecting her follower to walk right past.

He made the turn, as well.

She forced herself to breathe slowly, in and out, countering the patter of her heartbeat. People walked down the same streets all the time. She was being silly. Here she hadn't even had a sip of coffee and every nerve in her body felt like it was buzzing. Maybe she didn't need the extra jolt of caffeine after all. Maybe tonight she was twitchy enough without it.

The darkened tower of her family business loomed ahead. She walked a little faster in spite of herself. With any luck, the parking attendant would still be at his post. He would smile his usual friendly smile, and she would chuckle to herself about how paranoid she was being. She didn't know why she felt so afraid of a guy that just a moment ago she'd thought was kind of cute. Sure, when it came to choosing men, she was a horrible failure. But that didn't mean just because she glanced this guy's way he would turn out to be a mugger.

She passed the stairwell leading to the parking garage's lower level and made for the car entrance and the attendant. She turned the corner and looked to the booth.

It was empty.

Natalie's mouth went dry. She spun around, certain the man would be behind her, a gun in his fist or maybe a knife, his lips pulling back in a sinister smile.

The sidewalk was empty, as well.

She waited. Ten seconds. Twenty. No one appeared.

He must have turned off. He must not have been following her after all.

She was obviously losing her mind. Understandable, she supposed. Ever since Rick Campbell had been exonerated in her parents' murders two months ago and then was killed himself, the entire Kendall clan had been on edge. Murder did that. If any family knew that, it was theirs.

On top of that, two of her three brothers, Ash and Devin, had lived through horrors of their own in the past two months. Horrors they'd thankfully overcome. Both now engaged to women they loved, her two oldest brothers had been blessed as well as challenged. But the deaths of their parents continued to hang over the entire Kendall family like a shroud.

She shook her head to dislodge shadowy thoughts she'd been trying to banish for twenty years. As if a mere shake of the head would do that. The only thing that worked was painting. Turning her childhood fears and guilt into images. Getting them out of her head, onto canvas and shutting them away in her studio where no one could see them.

She ripped open the flap on her coffee and took a long sip. Already her heartbeat was slowing. Already she was starting to feel normal again. But despite her earlier promise to herself, she didn't feel much like laughing. All she felt was grateful no one else had witnessed her ridiculousness.

Replacing the coffee flap in order to keep her latte hot, she continued down the ramp to the garage's lower level. A lowered garage door and smaller human-size door nestled side by side at the bottom of the ramp. The executive parking filled the whole lower level. Besides being security locked, this part of the garage also had the advantage of being heated in the winter. And it had both a street entrance and an elevator that led directly to the offices on the upper floors.

Balancing her coffee in one hand, she groped in her bag for her keys.

The door behind her clicked open.

She whirled around.

Emerging from the stairwell was the man with the untucked shirt. The door slammed with a loud clang.

The sound shuddered up Natalie's spine and echoed off the concrete. For a moment, she couldn't focus. She couldn't move. All she could do was think about how alone the two of them were—no other cars, no one to come to her aid. Even if she screamed, would anyone hear?

Her phone. Instead of grabbing her keys, she pulled out her cell. She stared at the screen. Underground garage. Surrounded by concrete.

No service.

She held the phone to her ear anyway. If he thought she was calling someone, he would leave her alone. Wouldn't he? The shuffling sound of those god-awful loafers moved toward her.

A high whistle of panic rose in her ears. Oil and concrete and old exhaust clogged her throat.

"No reception down here, I bet," he said in a quiet voice.

He wasn't fooled by the phone. All she could do was make a run for it. Get through the door and slam it before he could follow. She dropped the useless phone back in her bag and groped for her keys. Her fingers hit steel. She pulled the key chain out, jingling in shaking fingers. She tried to fit her key into the lock.

"Need help with that?"

His voice was right behind her shoulder. The faint mint scent of mouthwash fanned her neck.

She turned her head to look at him.

He stared at her with sharp brown eyes. His dark blond hair was mussed, blown by the wind. He looked like a regular guy. Perfectly ordinary.

Then why was she so frightened?

She turned back to the door. He hadn't hurt her yet. Hadn't even touched her. All he'd done was ask if he could help. That had to mean something. Right? Maybe she was doing all this panicking for nothing. Maybe she really was going crazy after all. "No, thanks. I can get it."

"You seem…scared."

She didn't know what to say. Admit she was frightened out of her mind? Or just play it cool. "I was just startled."

"Startled? That's not what I had in mind."

His voice sounded low, calm. Everything Natalie wasn't. Everything she didn't think a mugger should be, either. "I'm…I'm okay now." She fibbed, feeling far less than okay.

He narrowed his eyes. "Do you know who I am?"

"Know you?" She turned to face him. He stood so close she took a step back, hitting the door. "You were in the coffee shop."

"Yes. I've been wanting to talk to you for a long time." He smiled. Cool. Casual. But his eyes…something about them seemed hard. Something about his smile felt less than friendly.

Was she imagining it?

"Excuse me. Hate to interrupt." The voice came from behind the man. Someone else.

She peered past one of the skinny shoulders. Another man stood in the doorway to the stairwell, his tall, well-muscled frame filling the space. Everything about him—the expression on his face, the way he held his body, the look in his eyes—exuded calm and control. And even though she didn't know anything more about this man than she did the guy who'd followed her from the coffee shop, she let a relieved breath escape from her lungs and sagged back against the door. "No interruption. Really."

The man staring at her turned to face the interloper. "Who in the hell are you?"

"I'd like to ask you the same question."

"Too bad I asked it first."

He walked from the stairwell. His steps came slow and steady but Natalie could feel something coiled underneath. Power. Readiness. He stopped a few feet away. His eyes focused on the smaller man, hazel slits. "I'm a friend of Ms. Kendall's. You?"

The man closest to her looked away to the door. His shoulders seemed to grow even more slight. He shuffled away from her, one step, two. "I'm… This is a misunderstanding."

She wasn't sure what was misunderstood. He hadn't said or done anything. Not really. Looking at him, Natalie couldn't quite remember why she'd felt so threatened. He seemed anything but threatening now.

"I think we understand each other just fine," said the second man. He ran a hand over his cropped, brown hair. "Now if you don't mind, I'd like a word with Ms. Kendall. Alone."

The thin man nodded and made for the

ramp Natalie had followed into the garage, shoulders hunched. He didn't look back.

As soon as he climbed out of sight, Natalie focused on the man in front of her. Of the two of them, he was definitely the strongest, physically the more threatening. He even knew her name, although she'd never seen him before. She was sure she hadn't. She'd remember. But despite the fact that she was alone and defenseless in the same position as she'd been with the other man moments ago, this time she felt inexplicably safe.

But, of course, taking her history with men into account, that was probably a bad sign. "So who are you? And how do you know my name?"

Chapter Two

As soon as Gray stepped from the stairwell, he knew this question would be coming. He also knew he didn't have an answer for it. Not one Ms. Natalie Kendall would like, anyway. If he wanted to follow his client's directions, he was going to have to lie. Or at least tweak the truth a little. He just hoped Natalie's brother was ready to cover his tracks. "Grayson Scott. Call me Gray."

She stared as if waiting for the rest.

"I work at your company."

A tiny crease dug between her eyebrows. "I'm sorry. I don't remember ever having met you."

"I just talked to Mr. Kendall about the job today."

The crease didn't fade. Her mouth dipped in a frown and she glanced off to the side, as if she knew what he was saying wasn't exactly the truth and she was conjuring a way to trip him up. "Which Mr. Kendall did you talk to?"

"The CEO, Devin Kendall." At least that answer was the truth. "He's your brother, correct?"

"Devin isn't looking to fill any vacancies. Not that he told me about."

He gave a shrug. "Kendall isn't a tiny company. Do you usually know about all vacancies?"

"Usually, yes."

He held her gaze, hoping he appeared to have nothing to hide. That was the problem with off-the-cuff lies. It was impossible to make sure your cover story held water. And stacking one lie on top of another tended to multiply the potential for leaks.

"What division?" she asked.

Best to stick as close to the truth as he could. "Security."

"That's convenient."

He didn't react. Part of selling a lie was resisting the urge to explain.

She pushed strands of her straight, blond hair back over her shoulder. "I happen to know we just hired a bunch of extra security people over the past couple of months. We don't need more."

"You'll have to ask your brother about

that." And he had to talk to Devin before she could.

"I will." She narrowed her eyes. "You're not a bodyguard of some kind, are you?"

He'd been hoping she wouldn't ask that precise question. The woman seemed to have pretty good lie radar. He sure hoped the acting skills he'd honed in his one-and-only grade school play performance would be enough to see him through.

He gave her an aw-shucks grin. "Nothing so glamorous, I'm afraid. I work with locks and alarm systems."

"Really?" She looked at him harder, if that was possible.

If she didn't blink soon, he was going to start to sweat. "You don't like locks and alarm systems?" he tossed off, hoping a little levity would help his case.

"I thought that was Glenn Johnston's area."

He'd figured a company like Kendall would already have locks and alarms covered, so he was ready with a twist. "I have a meeting with Glenn tomorrow. Your brother said he'd set it up. He wants to update to the newest technology. That's where I come in."

She crooked one eyebrow. "And Glenn is going along with this idea?"

"I haven't met him yet, so I have no clue."

Her face seemed to relax, one corner of her lips turning up slightly with amusement. "Good luck with that meeting."

"Don't tell me, Glenn's a technophobe." He gave her what he hoped was a worried expression. Hell, he was worried. He seemed to have chosen just the wrong cover story. He hoped it wouldn't be too tough for Devin to back up.

"He's a little resistant to new things, that's all. As long as Devin paves the way for you, it should be fine." She nodded, her mood shifting from suspicious to encouraging.

"Thanks for the heads-up on Glenn Johnston. It helps to know I should tread softly." So far, so good. Now to angle the conversation toward the subject he really wanted to address. "In the meantime, who was that guy you were talking to?"

She glanced at the ramp leading out of the garage, as if half expecting him to be waiting in the shadows. "I don't know."

"You've never seen him before?"

"Not before tonight. He was in the coffee shop I just left." She held up a large to-go cup with the logo of a nearby coffee shop emblazoned on the side. "He followed me."

"Why?"

She shook her head, looking a little lost. "I have no idea."

She really seemed at a loss. He fought the urge to reach out and rub his hand up and down her arm. Somehow he doubted she'd see the move as supportive coming from a guy she'd just met. "Did he say anything to you?"

"Not much. He asked if I knew him."

"Knew him?"

She gave a little shrug. "From the coffee shop, I guess."

"And you're sure you've never seen him before tonight?"

"I don't remember him. But he might have been there before. It's the closest coffee shop. I go there all the time. I like their lattes." She held up her cup again as if showing him proof. "Thank you, by the way. He really didn't do anything, and I'm not sure I actually needed saving, but I appreciate it anyway."

"Not a problem. I am joining the security crew tomorrow. Might as well get an early start on the job. Just glad I didn't have to install an alarm right on the guy's nose." He feigned giving the air an awkward punch.

She laughed, the sound tinkling off the concrete around them, frothy and fun and yet something deeper underneath.

He'd been following her for a while now, but he'd never been face-to-face like this and he'd never before heard her laugh. He'd like to hear more of it.

"Well, thank you. I really do appreciate you stepping in to help. There aren't a lot of Good Samaritans around these days." She started to angle her body away from him, suggesting it was time to go.

He nodded and smiled. Of course, he wasn't a Good Samaritan, although that was what he'd wanted her to believe. He was paid to stick his neck out. Even though this case hadn't required much stretching so far. "Let me see you to your car."

She flicked her eyes back to his, her expression carrying a hint of question but not the suspicion that had been there earlier. "That's not necessary."

"Yes, it is. I need to know you're safe. I couldn't live with myself if I just walked away and something happened to you."

She raised her chin as if she'd figured him out. "Because I'm the new boss's sister and an executive at Kendall?"

"No. I suppose that's a good reason, but it's not my primary one." Of course, technically protecting the boss's sister *was* his reason for being here, but the words felt good on his tongue.

She tilted her head to the side and arched her eyebrows as if waiting for him to come clean.

"Let's just say I'll be thinking about you all night. I don't want those thoughts to be laced with worry." It sounded like a line, and as soon as he'd said it he'd wanted it back. The ironic thing was it was one of the first honest things he'd said to her.

She smiled.

Despite the greenish flicker of the parking structure's fluorescent lights, he picked up a little more color in the apples of her cheeks. Encouraging. "So will you let me see you to your car?"

"I guess it wouldn't hurt." She looked down at the keys in her hand then returned her gaze to his. "But I'm having trouble with my keys. You're a Kendall employee. Security, even. Do you have yours?"

He could feel his grin from the inside out. "Testing me, huh?"

"Does that seem paranoid?"

"It seems smart." And luckily Devin had given him keys to the parking garage weeks ago. He pulled them out and made a show of unlocking the door. He held it open for her to pass through.

She shot him the kind of smile that had him thinking all sorts of things, none particularly protective. "Thank you." If he wasn't mistaken, there was a flirty lilt to her tone.

This job was getting a whole lot more interesting.

They walked side by side through the structure, the wide-open space feeling more intimate than it had a right to. He found himself thinking about leaning close, trying to detect a whisper of her scent over the odor of concrete and old exhaust. Of all the lies he'd told her tonight, the fact that he was attracted to her wasn't one. Ever since he'd started following her, he hadn't been able to help thinking of her—day and night—and not in a typical bodyguard sort of way. But none of those thoughts compared with being face-to-face.

Of course, he'd never intended to actually meet her. And now that he had, he found himself with a problem. For weeks he'd kept an eye on her without her noticing he was there. But after tonight, he had the feeling she'd notice, no matter how good his surveillance skills were. If he wanted to continue to perform as her bodyguard without her knowledge, he had to find some kind of reason to hang around.

And it seemed one had just landed in his lap. He just had to play it right.

A cherry-red sports car sat at the far end of the structure. Natalie pointed her remote at the car and the driver's door opened with a chirp. Hand on the door handle, she offered him a smile. "Thank you."

"Like I said, it's not a problem."

"Still, I appreciate your concern."

"Do you appreciate it enough..." He looked away. "No. Sorry. I think I'm flirting with overstepping my bounds."

"What were you going to say?" She looked straight at him with clear green eyes, as if she really wanted to know.

Just the response he was after. "You won't hold it against me?"

"After you saved me from the notorious coffee shop mugger? How could I?"

"Okay, I was just going to ask if you'd like to meet for lunch tomorrow."

Her smile grew to a full-fledged grin. "I think I could fit it in."

"Oh, Jolie, you're not going to wear *that,* are you?" Natalie tried to sound serious, but the look on Jolie's face made her bubbly good mood even better. She let loose with a smile, despite best intentions.

Jolie shot her a dry look. "It looks fabulous, doesn't it?"

Natalie skimmed her eyes over the one-shoulder peacock silk number. Jolie's red hair, creamy skin and green eyes looked unbelievable with the silk's rich color, and the dress itself looked like something straight off the red carpet. Natalie couldn't lie. Her friend and future sister-in-law looked breathtaking. "Devin is going to want to marry you on the spot."

Jolie laughed and held up a hand. "If he does, he's out of luck. You have to see Rachel's bridal gown."

Set to marry Natalie's notorious bachelor cop brother, Ash, Rachel was the bride-to-be. The reason she and Jolie were here. But Jolie had a rock on her finger that was twice as big as Rachel's and a wedding to Natalie's brother Devin to prepare for, as well. "I can't wait to see Rachel in her dress. I'm sure she looks gorgeous."

Jolie sashayed in front of the multiangle bridal shop mirror. "I want the whole wedding thing for myself, too. Including that white dress. For real, this time. No pretending."

Natalie nodded. As part of a plan to distract the media who had taken to following Devin's every move, Jolie and Devin had staged a fake engagement and pretended to plan their wedding. It had been tough on Jolie, who'd been in love with her boss for a long while. But in the end, she and Devin had both realized they wanted to be married.

For real.

On the other hand, Natalie only had bridesmaids' dresses in her future, and as fabulous as this one was, it didn't compare to the white, fairy-tale gowns.

But maybe…

A shimmer warmed her chest as she thought of how wonderful Gray would look in a tuxedo, waiting for her at the altar. She let out a sigh and tried to tamp down the fantasy, tough since she'd had her wedding planned out since she was about seven. It was definitely too soon for marriage plans, but at least she had a lunch date to look forward to.

"What are you so happy about?" Jolie stared at Natalie via her reflection.

"It's a great dress."

Jolie shot her a no-nonsense look. "That's not a dress smile. I know you. That's a man smile."

Natalie couldn't help but laugh.

"I knew it." Jolie turned away from the mirror and faced Natalie directly. "So spill. I just saw you at the office and your mood wasn't *this* fabulous. What happened?"

Natalie was far more excited than she should be to tell Jolie the story of how she met Gray.

Jolie reacted in all the right ways. She gasped at the image of Natalie being followed from the coffee shop. Her eyes widened when Natalie described the man emerging from the stairwell. And she let out a relieved breath at Gray's well-timed rescue.

Natalie paused for dramatic effect. "And my rescuer? He asked me out."

Jolie's lips flattened into a line.

Not the response Natalie was after. "I thought you'd be happy for me."

Jolie glanced away.

"What is it? You said yourself that I needed to meet different men. And this one is... wow."

"I wasn't thinking of some guy who suddenly appears in a parking garage."

"He works at Kendall."

Jolie's frown grew deeper. "How do you know that?"

"He said Devin hired him to be part of the

security department, and he had a key to the garage."

"Devin hired…" Jolie pulled in a long breath and shook her head. "Going out with him doesn't seem like a very good idea."

"You're not warning me about workplace romances, are you? You, of all people?" She never would have expected this kind of response from Jolie, who had just gotten engaged to Natalie's brother Devin…who also happened to be her boss.

"It just doesn't feel right, that's all. You don't know anything about him."

"I know he's nice and good-looking and he saved me from a guy who was a little bit creepy and wore really bad shoes."

Jolie normally would have laughed at a comment like that, but she didn't even crack a smile.

"I don't believe this. I thought you'd be happy for me."

"I just think you should be careful."

"Careful?"

"You have to admit, you've picked some losers."

"But Gray isn't like those other guys." Natalie couldn't even count the ways he was different.

"How do you know that?"

How *did* she know? "I don't know. I just do."

Once again, Jolie gave her head a slow shake. "He could be something totally different than what you think. You might really start to like him only to have him turn around and leave."

Like all those other guys...

Jolie hadn't said it, but she might as well have.

Natalie wanted to protest, but at the moment, the words were totally out of reach. If she was honest with herself, she had to admit Jolie was probably right. Her friend knew what kind of men she'd dated. She'd heard the horror stories, even witnessed some of Natalie's epic fails.

She tried her best to give Jolie a smile and plucked a gorgeous midnight-blue silk dress with a dramatic draped neckline from the rack. "You're right. He can't be as good as he seems."

Jolie tilted her head and offered an apologetic smile. "I'm sorry, Nat. I know you thought I'd be happy for you. I just don't want to see you hurt again."

She couldn't blame Jolie. "I know. I've done a good job of picking jerks over the years, haven't I?"

"It's not only that. You know, things have

so been…crazy. Call me paranoid, but I don't want any of that to rub off on you."

She understood where her future sister-in-law's worry was coming from. The Kendall family had faced enough danger in the past two months to make anyone a bit wary, even someone as plucky as Jolie. She and Devin had been through a lot and so had Ash and Rachel.

She gave Jolie a smile. "You don't have to worry about me."

"But I do."

"Well, stop it. I know things have been weird, but no one is going to want anything from me."

Jolie didn't look convinced.

"Really. Ash is a cop, Rachel a crime scene investigator and Devin is CEO of the company. Fair or not, they're going to make enemies. And with everything we believed about the past blowing up, they've had a lot to deal with. But no one is going to target someone like me. I'm not part of the investigation. I was only six years old when… you know, they died." She paused to take a breath. She didn't normally talk about her parents' twenty-year-old murders, not even to Jolie, and it took a second for her to compose herself and go on. "I have no power outside of the public relations department at Kendall Communications. I'm a threat to no one."

"I'm not so sure."

"I am. The biggest thing I have to fear is giving my heart to another man who'll stomp on it and throw it away." And in worrying about that, Jolie was right.

"Natalie?" Her future sister-in-law's voice was steeped in concern. "I didn't mean—"

"It's okay. I know I don't have the most reliable taste when it comes to men. But at least I do know my dresses, and this one that Rachel picked out for me is divine." She turned the hanger of the midnight-blue dress in her hand and the skirt flowed with the movement as if dancing on air.

Jolie tilted her head to the side and studied Natalie. From the look on her face, she wasn't falling for the dress distraction. "You're not going on the lunch date, are you?"

She didn't want to say the word, but she knew she had to. "No, of course not. That would be stupid."

"I'm glad. The whole situation feels weird to me. Especially now, with all that's been going on. I don't think you should risk seeing a guy who conveniently shows up out of the blue like that."

"I didn't say I wasn't going to see him again."

The warning was back in Jolie's eyes.

"I don't have his phone number, okay? I have to see him to tell him I'm not going to lunch."

"Natalie…"

"Don't worry. I'll just find him at the office tomorrow. Nothing bad will happen to me." She started for one of the tiny dressing stalls off the mirrored salon. "How about I try on this gorgeous dress, and we'll go see if we can find Rachel? I want to see that gown."

She closed the door behind her and leaned back against it just in time to hide the stupid tears brimming in her eyes.

Chapter Three

The barista raised a brow, the silver hoop skewering her flesh glinting in the coffee shop's warm lighting. "Why're you asking about Wade? He's harmless."

Gray didn't know about that. As soon as he'd left Natalie in the parking garage, he'd walked over to the coffee shop to get some information about the man who'd been following her. "Do you know his last name?"

She switched on the milk steamer and for a moment Gray couldn't make out a single word over the loud whirring and slurping sound of the machine.

Finally she set his cappuccino on the counter. "Will that be all?"

"Wade's last name?"

She rolled her eyes. "I said I didn't remember it. I'm not a damn directory."

"He followed a woman from this shop tonight. I want to determine if this could be a problem."

"Oh, her. Yeah, I saw that. He's been watching her for a couple weeks now. Every time they're in here together. Coffee shops are the new pickup spots, you know."

"You think he's trying to ask her out?"

She tossed him a shrug. "She often comes in after work, and he's here. Like he's waiting for her but can't get up the nerve to say hello. Like I said, he's harmless."

She might be right. He'd seemed nervous in the parking ramp earlier tonight, but there wasn't anything overtly threatening about him. Still he had to wonder about a guy who would follow a woman through the deserted downtown streets at night. If he wasn't trying to intimidate her, then he must be the most insensitive and clueless man on the planet. And that was saying something.

The bleat of his cell phone interrupted his next thought. He looked down at the display. Devin Kendall. Gray glanced up at the barista. "Thanks." He grabbed his cappuccino and held the phone to his ear. "Yes?"

"Jolie just called." The CEO's voice sounded curt and authoritative, as always. "They're getting ready to leave the bridal shop."

"Okay. I'm on my way back." He was about to end the call when Devin spoke again.

"What did you find out about the creep you said was following my sister tonight?"

He'd filled Devin in as soon as he'd seen Natalie safely inside the bridal shop. "A first name. Wade. Not much else. He could be just some aspiring Romeo."

"In Natalie's case, that's reason to worry."

Gray was curious about the statement, especially since he'd like to cast himself as that Romeo, but he resisted the urge to ask for the story behind the comment. Everything he knew about Devin Kendall suggested he was an overprotective big brother. Gray doubted he'd be eager to share stories about his sister's love life, especially with a hired bodyguard. "Don't worry, I have it under control. I'm heading back to the bridal shop now."

"Good. Don't let her see you this time."

"I think I've figured out a way to deal with that problem."

"Does this have something to do with wanting me to say I've hired you on as the new alarm system wunderkind on Kendall's security team?"

"That's part of it." Gray had decided to tell Devin all of his plan when he'd talked to him the first time. Now he wasn't sure he wanted to mention the rest in light of Devin's comments about Natalie and Romeos. At least not yet.

"Fine. Whatever your plan is, just make sure it works. I don't want to have to explain why I hired a bodyguard behind her back. She would be less than understanding." Devin hung up.

Gray stuffed his phone in his pocket. He had a short hike back to his car. He'd better hurry.

"I thought that was you."

He recognized her voice immediately. How could he not? Her words the day of her husband's funeral echoed in the back of his mind every night when he closed his eyes and every morning when he opened them. "Sherry." He turned around.

Her eyes glinted hard like shards of black glass and on her finger sparkled the ring she'd gotten from Jimbo, the man he always thought of as his brother. "You have a lot of nerve, coming back to St. Louis, Grayson."

He didn't know what to say to that. She was probably right. But as out of place as he now felt here, he didn't feel comfortable anywhere else, either. He couldn't spend his life running away. "It's my home, Sherry. Just like it's yours."

"And Jimbo's."

He nodded, his chest aching at the bitter edge in her voice. "Yes. And Jimbo's," he said in a quiet voice.

She blinked as if fighting tears and shook her short, dark hair. "I hear you got yourself a job as a bodyguard. What a laugh. Does your client know that you aren't the type to lay down his life for anyone?"

He stood straight as if taking a drill sergeant's abuse and met her eyes full on. "You're wrong."

"Wrong? No. If I was wrong, Jimbo would be here right now instead of at Jefferson Barracks National Cemetery. I wish I was wrong about you. I wish it every day."

The pain aching in her voice stole his breath. "I miss him, too, Sherry."

"Yeah, right."

He opened his mouth to protest, then shut it without speaking. Whatever he said wouldn't change how Sherry felt about him, what she thought she knew. He wasn't sure how she'd found him, but he could tell it wasn't an accident. She'd come looking for him. And she looked prepared to take a pound of flesh.

He blew out a breath, and it condensed into a cloud in the cold air. Truth was, he couldn't blame her. Whatever cruel words she wanted to hurl, he deserved them. He'd said worse to the reflection in his mirror. The bottom line was that one of the best men Gray had ever known had died and Gray hadn't. And if Jimbo's wife couldn't forgive him for that fact, she wasn't alone.

Gray couldn't forgive himself, either. "I'm so sorry, Sherry, but I have to go."

"Don't want to face the truth?"

He shook his head. He felt for Sherry. And he missed Jimbo, his friend, his brother. If he could change things, he would. But right now, the best thing he could do was steer clear and focus on his job. He had to get back to the bridal shop before Natalie left. He couldn't change the past, but he could shape the future. His future. His redemption.

And it all started with keeping Natalie Kendall safe.

NATALIE WAS RELIEVED when she finally pulled her car through the gate surrounding the Kendall Estate, the iron scrollwork closing securely behind her. It used to be that her aunt and uncle often didn't bother to close the gate. They just left it open, the quiet upscale neighborhood giving them little reason to worry about security. But with all the trouble the family had been having, that practice had changed.

She looked up at the traditional gray stone mansion and let out a long, relieved breath. Maybe it was the strange run-in with the guy who'd followed her from the coffee shop, or maybe it was Jolie's mistrust of Gray, but she could have sworn a car had followed her home from the bridal shop.

She let her car idle in the driveway and eyed the street through the tall fence. The street was quiet. No headlights. No car creeping past, slowing down to see where she'd turned. Nothing.

Maybe she was losing her mind.

She shifted her sports car into gear and continued past the main house where her aunt and uncle lived. She'd grown up in the Kendall mansion, and living inside its walls still made her feel like a child. That was why, after she'd returned from college, she'd moved into the guest cottage in the rear of the estate. It was easier to deal with the memories if she wasn't living them every day.

Of course, all that had happened the past two months had brought those memories out, front and center. And even her little house among the gardens couldn't hide her from them.

She followed the winding drive past the pool house and rose garden and cove of evergreens until she reached her cottage, nestled among tall oaks. On the verge of shedding their leaves, the trees reached twisted limbs into the night sky. A scene that reminded Natalie far too much of Halloween horrors.

Or much worse, the real kind.

She parked in her little garage and let herself into the house. She loved her cottage. With only two bedrooms, one she'd transformed into an art studio, the place was cozy, warm on nights like these, and safe. At least it always had felt that way.

Now every part of her life felt uneasy.

She switched on the light and stepped into the kitchen. The window over the sink stared at her like an unblinking eye. She pulled the blinds, crossed her arms over her chest and tried to rub warmth through the jacket sleeves.

She was being ridiculous, freaking herself out this way. And over nothing. Sleep. That's what she needed. A good night's sleep and the morning light would make the world look much different. Tomorrow she would be able to put everything back into perspective. The man who'd followed her…Gray…Jolie's nerves…she just needed sleep.

She passed through the dinette and the living area, turned down the hall to the bedrooms and shivered, despite herself. A draft seemed to be moving in this part of the little house. She switched on the hall light. The flow of air seemed to be coming from her studio. Strange. And the door stood open.

A door she always kept locked.

Her heartbeat launched into double time. She reached out a hand and pushed the door open farther. Curling her arm around the doorjamb, she felt for the light switch and flicked it on.

At first she wasn't sure what she was seeing. Shreds of canvas hung from her work easel. Red paint pooled on the floor. The glow of the moon sparkled on shattered glass.

A gasp caught in her throat, and she turned to run.

Chapter Four

"Here you go, dear." Angela Kendall pushed a mug of tea into Natalie's hands, plopped down on the kitchen chair next to her and studied her niece with concerned brown eyes. "It will calm you, make you feel better."

Natalie wrapped both palms around the hot mug, grateful to have something to hold on to that would help to steady her shaking hands. The scent of chamomile wafted toward her. The tea her aunt pulled out to soothe any trauma Natalie faced, from her love life woes to the nightmares she'd had since she was six.

Natalie hated chamomile tea.

Aunt Angela leaned toward her, the kitchen light glinting off the few strands of gray that threaded her brown hair. "Is the tea all right, honey?"

"It's great." Natalie gave her aunt what she hoped was a grateful smile and dutifully lifted the tea to her lips. She took a sip of the dreadful brew and then returned the cup to the table. "Thank you."

Angela gave her a smile and ran her hand over Natalie's arm in a comforting caress. When Natalie had burst into the main house in a panic after finding the broken window and slashed paintings in her cottage, her aunt had been wearing her bright pink bathrobe and matching pajamas, ready for bed. Somewhere between soothing Natalie, alerting Uncle Craig and brewing tea, she'd changed into an orange sweater and jeans, combed her hair smooth and dashed on a bit of mascara and tinted lip balm.

The woman was nothing short of amazing.

Natalie was lucky to have her, back when she was six and her aunt and uncle had taken in orphaned Natalie and her three older brothers as their own and now. But as much as she appreciated her aunt's nurturing, this much coddling made Natalie feel as if she was once again a weak, traumatized little girl.

Uncle Craig walked back into the kitchen before Aunt Angela had a chance to urge Natalie to take another sip. "Ash is bringing a couple of patrol officers with him."

So now the whole St. Louis Police Department was going to get involved? Natalie supposed it made sense, but she still felt like hiding her face. "I'm sorry for all this."

"Sorry? Why should you be sorry?" Uncle Craig's eyes flashed blue fire. "You didn't break into your own cottage and vandalize it. The person who did this, that's who should be sorry."

"That's right, dear," Aunt Angela chimed in. "How long before Ash gets here?"

"He was getting into the car when I hung up."

The grandfather clock down the hall chimed loud and slow.

Natalie glanced around the kitchen. The room was immaculate, as usual. Beautiful cabinets, gleaming countertops, and just the right decorating touches. Yet nothing was stuffy or showy. She didn't remember much about the house when her parents lived here, but since her aunt and uncle had moved in to take care of Natalie and her brothers, the house had felt like Angela. Warm, well cared for, welcoming.

She choked down another sip of tea for her aunt's sake. She hated being so needy, so clingy. She wanted to feel strong for once in her life, confident that she could stand on her own feet. That she could love as an equal and have that love returned. She wanted to forget that night twenty years ago. That night that chewed at the back of her mind.

Before she knew it, Ash was striding into the kitchen. He wore jeans and a simple shirt. A leather jacket spanned his broad shoulders and muscular chest. With his light brown hair, glinting green eyes and confident swagger, it was no wonder he had been known as the Casanova of the St. Louis PD. That is, until he fell hard for Rachel and their unborn child and realized all he really wanted was to settle down.

He immediately crossed to Natalie. "You okay?"

The concern in his voice made her throat feel thick. She managed a nod.

"Uncle Craig said someone broke into the cottage?"

"That's right," Craig answered.

Natalie forced her voice to function and filled her brother in on how she'd sensed the draft and found her studio door open and the window shattered.

"Did you notice if anything was missing?" he asked when she'd finished.

"I don't know. I ran out." She had. Like a scared little girl.

"You did the right thing. There's always a chance the intruder could have still been there. When the squad car gets here, I'll go out and take a look around."

Her throat closed. The paintings. She hadn't even thought about the fact that her brother and his fellow officers would need to investigate. And when they did, they'd see the shreds of her canvases littering the floor.

Would Ash realize what the images were? Was she ready for him to see what she'd been painting?

"Is that okay?" He narrowed his green eyes.

She forced a nod.

"What's wrong?"

The disadvantage of having a cop for a brother. He could sense when she wasn't being totally up front. "Nothing. I'm just a little shaken."

"You can stay here tonight, honey. In fact, you can move back in. We'd love to have you. You know that."

She gave her aunt her best attempt at a smile. Her aunt and uncle were the only parents she'd ever really known. Sure she had images of her mother and father. But she'd only been six when they died. And the images she had of them were all mixed up with memories of the Christmas morning she'd awakened, excited about seeing what

Santa brought her, and instead had discovered her parents' murdered bodies.

"A squad car just pulled into the drive. Oh, here comes Devin, too."

Natalie almost groaned. With her aunt and uncle, Ash and Devin all hovering over her, all she was missing was her third brother, Thad. Of course, she was sure he'd be here, too, if he wasn't on assignment as a photo-journalist in some remote locale. He probably hadn't even heard about all that had happened in St. Louis the past couple of months. They'd tried to reach him to tell him their parents' murderer had been exonerated, but hadn't been able to find him. Devin had left a message with a woman at the news network, but they hadn't heard a word since.

Another concern to add to the rest.

"We'll handle this. You don't worry." Ash gave her a quick hug and headed for the door.

To her studio...

"Ash, wait. Can I talk to you?" She had to prepare him for what he would find.

He turned around and paused, as if he expected her to start talking right there in front of her aunt and uncle.

"In the study?" She tried not to notice the slightly hurt expression from her aunt.

Ash motioned for her to lead the way. Once

he shut the door behind them, he turned to her with a spill-it-all look he'd mastered long before he'd become a cop.

Natalie's throat felt dry as sawdust. "The paintings in my studio...I just wanted to warn you..." She tried to swallow.

"Your nightmares?"

She nodded.

"I should have known they'd come back after all that's happened the past two months. You should have told me."

"It's not so bad. Not as long as I paint them, to get them out of my head." She hadn't told him to elicit his concern. God knew, she had plenty of that. "The paintings were slashed. I wasn't in the house long, but I didn't notice anything else damaged."

"Just those paintings..."

"Do you think it means anything?"

"Maybe. Maybe not. I'll take a look around."

He hadn't answered her question, but that was as good as an answer with Ash. If he could have told her this had nothing to do with their parents' murders, he would have.

"Don't worry. You're safe now. Go upstairs. I'm sure Aunt Angela has your old room ready for you. Get some sleep and we'll get to the bottom of this. It will be all over before you know it, and the situation will be back to normal."

She pressed her lips together. Not a smile but as close as she could get. Even though she knew he was right, that she was safe, she couldn't help feeling this mess wasn't over.

No, she suspected it was just beginning.

"So NEEDLESS TO SAY, I didn't sleep much."

Gray leaned his elbows on the too-small café table and tried his best to seem shocked by Natalie's story. Of course, he'd followed her to the cottage from the bridal shop last night just as he followed her home every night. He'd been just about to go home himself and get some sleep when he'd seen her bolt from her cottage and dash to the main house where her aunt and uncle lived. It hadn't taken long for Devin to call him on his cell and demand answers Gray didn't have. Minutes after that, Natalie's cop brother, Ash, had squealed into the drive, eventually followed by a squad car and Devin himself.

It had been a long night for all of them.

"I'm sorry for laying this on you."

"What do you mean? I had to drag it out of you." He had. And he felt bad about it. But since he knew the events of the night before, he was afraid he'd slip up unless he convinced her to tell him herself. This way, he didn't have to keep as many details straight. And he had a seemingly legitimate reason to worry about her and insist he stay close.

The waitress swooped in on their table, deposited the check and two cups of coffee and removed the remnants of their lunch, panang chicken for her, pad see ew for him. It had been a stellar lunch, great Thai food and even better company. The time had gone far too fast. Gray could see making lunch with Natalie a daily ritual. The only thing that could make it better would be not having to worry about keeping his cover story intact. "Did you stay the night at your parents' house?"

"Aunt and uncle. Although they raised us. Especially me."

Of course, he already knew her family history, and he felt guilty at once for causing her pain, especially in service of his subterfuge. "That's right. Your parents…they've been in the news lately. I'm sorry."

She waved his apology away, but a sadness touched her eyes that suggested she couldn't so easily dismiss the memories of her parents' murders.

Not surprising. Who could?

She sipped her coffee, then leaned back in

her chair, playing with a spoon still on the table. "You know, it's funny."

"Funny?"

She shrugged a shoulder as if trying to convince herself as well as him that what she was about to say was no big deal. "Funny that I've never felt comfortable talking about this."

"I'm sorry." Another dose of guilt. "I didn't mean to make you uncomfortable. We can talk about something else."

"No, that's the funny part."

He shook his head. "I'm not following."

"I don't feel uncomfortable. Not when I'm talking to you. Is that weird?"

"I don't know if it's weird. I think it's kind of nice." He reached across the table and took her hand before he thought to stop himself.

She accepted his touch, curling her fingers around his. "Me, too. My family likes to hover. Sometimes they act as if I'm six years old all over again."

Six was a young age to lose one's parents. He gave her hand a squeeze he hoped she'd read as understanding and not hovering. "It probably helps that I didn't know you when you were six. You don't seem to need hovering now."

A smile curved over her lips and sparkled into her eyes.

Suddenly *hovering* was at the bottom of his list. Tasting those lips, watching her eyes sparkle with passion when he kissed her... he took a sip of black coffee and focused on a colorful painting on the wall behind her. "Did the police find anything last night?"

"A mess." She shook her head. "My brother Ash is a detective. He, Devin and a couple other officers were out there half the night, but..."

"Nothing?"

"I can't figure it out. Why would someone want to destroy my paintings? I mean, these aren't great works of art. I don't show them or sell them or anything. It's just my pastime, you know?"

He knew more than she could guess. And one of the things he knew was she was more than a hobby artist. She might head up Kendall's PR department now, but she'd been a serious artist in college. When it came to looking for someone who would want to shred her paintings, maybe that was a place to start. "You've never had offers to show your work? Never had art lovers looking to buy?"

She tilted her head to the side. "A few. But

that's when I was doing more commercial stuff. These paintings were just for me."

"Just for you, huh? So you don't show them to anyone?"

"No. No one would be interested anyway."

"I have trouble believing you haven't had interest."

"One dealer who liked some of my previous work has asked. But I told him no."

Interesting. "Who was that?"

"It's not important. I'm not going to show them to him, let alone sell them."

He would have to find out who this dealer was, although he wasn't sure how to go about that at the moment. He sensed if he badgered her about a name, she'd get suspicious. He didn't want to ruin the easy rapport that had bloomed between them. But there was another thing he was curious about. "So I can talk you into letting me have a peek?"

She looked at him out of the corner of her eyes. "What, are you a secret art collector?"

"No. But I have a certain interest in the artist. I've heard looking at an artist's work is the best way to get to know her." He knew it sounded like he was playing her, but he wasn't. Not really. The truth was, he really was interested in seeing Natalie's paintings. He was interested in learning everything about her. At least everything he hadn't already seen by following her around for the past month or so.

Maybe that was his fascination. Nothing had happened in the past weeks. Natalie shopping. Natalie going to and from work. Maybe his thirst for a bit more adventure than this was fueling his need to get closer to her. Or maybe he'd spent so much time watching her, he was developing a bit of a crush. Either way, this was the most alive he'd allowed himself to feel in a long time. "What do you say? Will you show me?"

"That's a pretty intimate request for a first date."

"Did I cross a line?"

She gave him a little smile. "No harm in asking."

"I could think of a more intimate request." He didn't even hope she would grant him what was in his imagination right now, but he didn't try to hide the interest in his voice.

"Can you? And what would that be?" She looked at him straight on, a mischievous glint in her green eyes.

He almost shook his head. "Man, I love a woman who ups the ante."

She arched her brows. "Well?"

He was tempted to tell her exactly where

his thoughts were leading, but he sensed that might be pushing things too far. He couldn't afford to come on too strong and risk scaring her off.

Or even worse, she might take him up on the offer. He could just imagine what her brother's reaction to that would be. "No harm in asking."

She laughed, the sound drawing him in as it had in the parking garage. If this was a real date, he'd lean over and kiss her. He could imagine how she'd taste. Sweet and light and spiced with Thai curry and a touch of coffee.

Instead of giving in to the urge, he grabbed the check folder off the table. "I would like you to let me buy."

"That's your intimate request?"

"Not intimate enough?"

She canted her head to the side. "I have an expense account here. And no, letting you buy lunch is not all that intimate."

"Sorry to disappoint." He slipped cash into the folder and handed it to a passing server. Then he looked into Natalie's cool, green eyes. "Okay, if you want something more intimate, may I escort you home after work tonight?"

"To see my paintings?"

"To make sure you get there safe and no one is waiting inside."

"Really?"

"After last night? Yeah, really. I'm worried about you."

"You hardly know me."

"True. But what I know, I really like. I want you to stay safe so I can get to know more."

She picked up her coffee cup and gave him a smile over the rim, as if he'd said precisely the right thing.

THE ENTIRE WALK BACK to Kendall Communications, Natalie mentally pinched herself. Since the moment she'd opened her studio door and found the room in shambles, she'd felt so violated, so vulnerable, she didn't think she'd ever feel strong and happy again. All night she'd been convinced someone was watching her from the darkness outside, even though the estate had been swarming with police. She could have sworn someone was trailing behind her on this morning's commute to work. She'd even felt the hair on the back of her neck rise while she was waiting for the parking ramp's garage door to open. So how was it possible that she felt so carefree and radiant after a simple chat over lunch?

Love was an incredible thing.

She turned away from Gray for a moment and smiled to herself. She wasn't in love, of course. She knew she was getting ahead of herself. Way ahead. But it was nice just to entertain the fantasy for a moment. To have found someone who made her feel giddy and warm and safe and sexy all at once. To have a future before her filled with love and family and happiness like Devin and Ash did. To plan her own wedding and know her husband would be there to share coffee with her in the evening and hold her warm and safe all night.

An old dream. Maybe an impossible one. But a good one all the same.

Jolie's warning flitted through her mind. She'd promised her friend she would call off today's lunch with Gray. But when it came down to telling him she had to cancel, she'd changed her mind. She was glad she had, despite having now lied to her best friend. Sure, Jolie was probably right. Sure, Natalie didn't really know Gray. Sure, her fantasies could come crashing down at any moment. But at least the dream would last over the lunch hour. After last night's trauma, she needed to hold on to this great feeling as long as she could. "So, we've talked a lot about me during lunch. Tell me about yourself."

Gray chuckled. "Believe me, you're a lot more interesting."

"I can't help liking that you think so, but beyond the trauma of last night, I'm afraid my life is pretty dull."

"There is nothing about you that's dull."

She let out a laugh. "You flatter," she said dryly.

He shot her a smile.

They reached the end of the block, and Gray held out his hand, preventing her from stepping into the street without him checking it out first. Natalie had to admit that if one of her brothers had made that move, she probably would have felt he was hovering. From Gray, it made her feel nothing but special. "I have to admit, compared to having my cottage broken into, dull is looking pretty appealing."

"I'm with you there. I'm just relieved you weren't hurt."

Footsteps shuffled behind them. Natalie resisted the urge to spin around and look. She shouldn't have brought up last night's break-in. Just a single mention and she was back to hearing things and feeling threats where none existed. She was walking down a public street, for crying out loud. Not only that, but anyone would be a fool to mess with the strapping man beside her, at least in a violent sort of way. Now, in a sexual way...

"What's so funny?"

Oh, God, she'd been grinning at her own joke. "Nothing."

"You sure about that? It looked a lot more interesting than nothing. And not dull at all."

She let out a giggle despite herself. She sounded like a teen with a crush. Hell, she felt like one, too. And she had to admit, it was kind of divine.

"Beautiful," Gray said under his breath.

Now it was her turn to be confused. She shot him a look. "What's beautiful?"

"The sound of your laugh. I like it. I want to hear more of it."

She laughed again. "You're just being sweet."

He gave her a playful wink. "On you? Maybe a little."

She wanted to hold on to his words. To run them through her mind and focus on the warm feeling spreading through her chest.

Man, she wished she'd met Gray years ago. Or at least a couple of months ago, back when her life felt more normal. This lunch hour would be perfect if not for the anxiety humming along her nerves like the buzz of a mosquito she couldn't swat.

She could still sense the person behind her, still there, still walking too close. Turning her head to the side, she caught a reflection in a store window. A powder-blue sweatshirt, large and slumpy enough to land whoever was wrapped in it a spot on *What Not to Wear*.

Natalie shook her head and directed her attention to the busy intersection ahead. The chrome exterior of the Kendall building rose over the surrounding cityscape, nearly blinding in the bright sun. Only one more block and her lunch with Gray would be over. There must be something wrong with her. A riveting man by her side dishing out compliments, and all she could focus on was paranoia and some woman's bad fashion choices.

They reached the end of the block and stopped at the crosswalk.

"What is it?" Gray glanced around.

She shook her head. "It's nothing."

He gave her a relaxed smile, scanning the cityscape. "You sure?"

His muscles were tense, alert, but Natalie sensed a strange calm coming from him that belied her jumpy nerves. "Yeah, I'm sure. I'm just being paranoid."

"In light of what happened to you last night, I don't think you can call it paranoia."

"That's nice of you to say."

"I mean it. You feel scared, whether you think it's real or not, you just let me know. Okay? I'm here for you."

A flutter lodged under her rib cage. He really was too good to be true. Something she'd have to keep in mind. She gave him a smile. "Thanks."

"Being here for you is not a problem. Trust me." He looked straight into her eyes.

A flush of heat started to pool in her cheeks. The mix of brown and green of his irises mesmerized her. The sincerity in his expression made her ache to step into his arms. She looked at the cars streaming past, not wanting him to see her melt. The curb under her toes felt like a cliff, one step and she'd be head over heels. And despite the fact that she didn't know Gray well, despite Jolie's warnings, despite all the disappointments she'd weathered in the past, Natalie was tempted to look back into his eyes and let herself fall.

Something hit her hard in the back and shoved her forward, into the street. She hit the pavement hard, the force jarring her knees and shuddering up through the heels of her hands.

All around her tires screeched and cars swerved.

Chapter Five

Gray didn't think, he didn't breathe, he just moved. He dashed into the street. Reaching Natalie, he grabbed her by the waist and lifted.

Drivers hit the brakes. Cars and trucks swerved as if skating on ice.

Gray backpedaled, half pulling, half carrying Natalie with him. His heel hit the curb and he fell backward onto the sidewalk. He hit the concrete on his back, rounding his spine and rolling up to his shoulders to absorb the impact and prevent his skull from hitting the hard surface. Natalie landed on his stomach, knocking the breath from his lungs.

For a second, he just held her, just struggled to breathe. He couldn't begin to process what had happened. One second they were talking, the next Natalie was flying into the street, traffic bearing down.

"Oh...oh..."

He could feel the sounds she made more than he could hear them. He loosened his grip and struggled to a sit. "Are you all right?"

Her skin was pale, her green eyes wide with shock. She stared at him, mouth open, but no words came.

"Natalie?"

"You saved me."

"It's my job."

"What?"

He shook his head. He needed to think before he talked. After following her for weeks, he hadn't really believed she was in danger. He'd allowed himself to grow complacent, paying more attention to how Natalie looked and what she was wearing than his surroundings. He was lucky he'd been walking so close beside her. If he'd still been merely watching her from a distance, she'd now be lying battered and bloody on the pavement. "I said I'd watch out for you. I meant it."

She let out a little puff of air.

Lips parted like that, adrenaline blasting through his body, he had a nearly overwhelming urge to kiss her.

Talk about inappropriate. "Let's get you off the street."

She looked around her, as if just remembering where she was, what had just happened. "She pushed me."

"Pushed you?" That would explain a lot. He looked around. An older couple strolled arm in arm about a half block away. Three executive types argued with waving arms as they stepped out of a nearby restaurant. A handful of pedestrians were scattered on the opposite side of the street. No one was anywhere near them, certainly not close enough to give Natalie a shove. "Who did it?"

"A woman. She was following right behind us. It had to be her."

"A light blue sweatshirt?"

Natalie nodded. "I saw her reflection in the store window."

"Did you recognize her?"

"I didn't see her face. Only the baggy sweatshirt. I didn't really get much of a look at her at all."

"Me, either." Some bodyguard he was. All these weeks of no activity had lulled him. He'd been so distracted by Natalie's laugh, by flirting with her, by his own damn fantasies that he hadn't paid blue-sweatshirt woman much attention at all. It had been his job to notice any threats to Natalie, and she'd gotten as good a look as he had.

His arms were still around Natalie, and he could feel her body begin to shake.

"Come on." He could beat himself up for his self-centeredness later. Right now, he wanted Natalie behind friendly walls. Preferably concrete ones.

Hurrying beside him, Natalie fished in her bag and pulled out her BlackBerry. "I'll call Ash."

"What are you going to tell him?"

"I don't know. She could walk up to me right now, and I wouldn't recognize her." She started to move the handheld back toward her purse.

"No, make the call. Please. Even if we can't tell him what she looked like, he needs to know what's going on." Gray would also have to fill Devin in on the situation. He doubted either brother would be surprised at the attack. They'd been worried about it, bracing for it. It had been him who was caught flat-footed.

Natalie finished leaving a message on Ash's voice mail by the time they reached the front entrance of Kendall Communications and ducked inside. A little late for lunch hour, the building felt still. The airy atrium smelled of delicious food and floor wax. Only a few diners remained in the café, probably shoppers enjoying a quiet afternoon in the public restaurant. He glanced up at the twenty-foot trees overhead. The place felt like a quiet garden cove, not the busy building it was, most employees in their offices organizing for their afternoon schedules, he supposed. They made it through the lobby and to the elevator bank. Almost the moment they arrived, a door opened.

The elevator car was empty. At least that worked out in their favor. He preferred alone, especially since he didn't know where any danger might be coming from. He ushered her inside and took what seemed like his first deep breath since he'd seen her flying into the street.

Soft music drifted in the air. Natalie hit the button that would take them to her sixteenth-floor office and looked up at him. Her face was still pale, but she had pulled herself together remarkably well for a civilian untrained in dealing with life-and-death stress. "It's amazing how you handled that."

"Amazing? Not really." She held out her scraped palms. Her fingers trembled visibly.

He reached out his own hands and gently folded hers in his. "I'm sorry I didn't notice that woman. I should have."

"For crying out loud, Gray. It's not your fault. You have nothing to be sorry about."

He did, but he couldn't see what good belaboring his apology would do. "I'm just so glad you're okay."

"I'm only okay because of you." She slipped her hands from his. But instead of stepping away from him, she moved closer. She looped her arms around his shoulders. She looked up at him, lips slightly parted. As she had out on the sidewalk and yet…different. Not desperation and fear this time, but desire.

Close calls stoked the libido, he knew that. Danger. Sex. In circumstances like this, one twisted into the other. But although reason niggled somewhere in the back of his mind, he didn't want to listen. He'd spent a lot of time reading those lips all the times he'd watched over her when she didn't know he was there. He wanted to taste them.

He dipped his head and fitted his mouth over hers.

She tasted like exotic spices. But underneath there was something sweeter, warmer, a flavor that was purely Natalie Kendall. He wanted more.

He knew he shouldn't do it, but he pulled

her close against his chest and delved deeper into the kiss.

A sound cut through the elevator music. The chime announcing they'd reached their floor. The whoosh of the door opening.

"Natalie."

Gray recognized the voice. He forced himself to release Natalie and end the kiss.

Then he turned to face Devin Kendall.

NATALIE HAD HAD A BAD DAY. Two bad days, really. Having her home violated last night seemed like child's play compared to being almost run over by cars today. She was shaking. Her knees and hands ached. And her beautiful new trousers were smudged with dirt and dust and one of the knees looked tattered. Now her only joy was being taken away from her by her big, overprotective brother.

She was less than happy. She was downright annoyed. "Hello, Devin."

"Ash called." Devin peered down at her, projecting his best stern, big brother look. Almost as tall as Gray, everyone always said he resembled their father almost exactly. But as stern as Devin came off sometimes, and as mad as she was at him now, Natalie always felt how much he cared for her. So much he came close to smothering her at times.

Times like right now. "So you know what happened. I hope Ash also told you that Gray pulled me out of the street. He saved me."

Devin didn't spare Gray a glance. He motioned to the inside of the elevator. "Is that was *this* is about?"

Natalie raised her chin. She was not in the mood for this. "If you must know, I was the one who kissed Gray."

Devin shifted his shoes on the floor. He finally pulled those sharp, blue eyes off Natalie and focused on Gray. "I need to talk to you."

Natalie resisted the urge to physically step between the men. Devin wouldn't dare fire Gray over this. At least she hoped not. But she was pretty sure he was set on embarrassing her. "You'd better not be planning to lecture Gray about kissing me," she warned. "It's none of your business, Devin."

"I need to talk to him about security matters. Alarms and such," Devin said in a flat voice.

Right. She opened her mouth to speak.

"I'll be right there, Mr. Kendall," Gray said before she could get out another word. "As soon as I see Natalie to her office. After what happened out on the street, I don't want to take any chances."

Natalie's heart gave a little hop. Devin wasn't her dad, and she was no teenage girl, but Gray's respect for Devin, yet polite defiance for her sake, thrilled her far more than it should.

If she wasn't so stressed over what had happened last night and on the street, and if Devin wasn't glaring at them right now, she'd be tempted to try for another kiss.

And she'd make it a doozy.

By the time he walked Natalie to her office, took the elevator to the twenty-fourth floor and made the trek to the executive office suite, Gray was ready for whatever the CEO had to throw at him.

At least he hoped he was.

The door had barely shut when the first words erupted from Devin Kendall's mouth. "What the hell do you think you were doing?"

Gray stepped over to the leather chairs in front of Devin's impressive desk and lowered himself into one. He might send other employees quivering with that commanding tone, but he'd have to try harder with Gray. Nothing could beat the drill sergeant he'd had in basic training. That guy could shout paint off walls and fur off puppies.

Devin stood up and pushed back his desk chair. He gave Gray a quiet glare, eyes like blue lasers. "Kissing my sister is not part of your job description."

Gray gave a nonchalant nod. Couldn't argue with that.

"Jolie told me about your lunch plans today. What kind of game are you playing here?"

"No game."

"Really? That doesn't jibe with what Jolie said."

Jolie, Devin's fiancée. One of the women Natalie met at the bridal shop last night. Natalie must have told her about their lunch plans. He'd love to know what else Natalie might have said.

"I hired you to be Natalie's bodyguard, not some kind of boyfriend. I want you to stay away from her."

"And how am I going to justify watching her? She's seen me now. Talked to me. That's going to make it a lot tougher to keep her from noticing that I'm following her. If we're dating, I have a built-in excuse to be near her. I can more effectively protect her." He eyed Devin. "It's the only story I could come up with that would allow me to stay near her without her suspecting the truth. Of course, that wouldn't be a problem if you'd just tell her you've hired a bodyguard."

"No."

"Why not? She doesn't need you to coddle her like this. She's a grown woman, not a little girl. Tell her the truth."

The CEO shook his head and paced across his office. "You don't know Natalie. She won't cooperate. Even after what's happened these past two days, she'll still maintain she doesn't need a bodyguard. She'll think I'm being overprotective." He rolled his eyes as he passed Gray's chair.

"Aren't you?"

Devin spun around.

Gray held up a hand. "I don't mean hiring a bodyguard is overprotective. Obviously something is going on here. But you should tell her. She'll deal with it."

Devin blew out a hard breath of air and shook his head. "I see she's told you how controlling I am."

"Not controlling. Overprotective. And it's not just you. She says she gets the same treatment from her brother Ash. And Thad, when he's back in the States."

"Did she tell you why?"

"No." But he found himself really wanting to know. "Care to fill me in?"

Devin shook his head and resumed pacing. "She just had a hard time when she was a girl, that's all."

He assumed Devin was referring to The Christmas Eve Murders. Gray had been only a teenager when it happened, but he remembered the stories about Joseph and Marie Kendall's deaths. It had shocked the community. St. Louis was a pretty big city. It saw its share of murders, but rarely were the victims part of the wealthy elite. And rarely did violence come to upscale neighborhoods like Hortense Place. The tragedy had been all over the news, and the recent developments in the case had consumed the media, as well. "Natalie was awfully young when your parents died."

"She was."

Seconds ticked by. Apparently Devin wasn't going to say more. Unlike his blustering first approach, the CEO seemed to draw into himself, as if he was watching Gray, carefully considering his next move.

Gray had the distinct feeling he'd underestimated Devin Kendall.

Finally the CEO spoke. "So what do you want? Besides my blessing to date my sister?" he asked in a tone that suggested a glacier would cover St. Louis before that would happen.

"I want you to either tell her I'm her bodyguard, or let me come up with my own cover story. Lucky for you, the second option is already under way."

"Lucky for me. Right."

Gray probably shouldn't say any more. Devin could fire him any moment and hire another bodyguard, one Natalie wouldn't recognize. But despite that risk, Gray knew he had to speak. Sometime in the past two days, the job had stopped being the important thing for him. Sometime Natalie had taken the number one spot. "For the record, I think she should know the truth. It would make things easier on all of us."

Devin paced to the window and stared out at the city below. The sun streamed in through the window, turning the rich brown of his hair to milk chocolate. His shoulders hunched, holding so much tension it was visible. He unbuttoned his jacket and stuffed his hands in the pockets of his expensive slacks. "This family has been through too much. Not just over the past couple of months, but the past twenty years. It's my job to make sure nothing else happens, that no one else gets hurt."

It seemed as if they'd already been over that ground. "I understand that."

Devin let out a heavy breath. "You'd better make sure Natalie doesn't fall in love with you. She's had far too much pain and sadness in her life. I don't want to be responsible for another bastard breaking her heart."

Chapter Six

After the traffic incident, several days passed without anything notable happening. The bruises on Natalie's knees and hands turned from angry red to purple to an ugly yellow. A glitch with a local bakery had left Rachel scrambling to find a new baker to make her wedding cake. Natalie had the nightmare nearly every night and had used the early-morning hours to restock her collection of paintings she'd never show. But other than the creepy feeling that someone was watching her now and then, nothing bad or dangerous or even that unusual happened.

Gray hadn't even kissed her.

She couldn't see Devin scaring him off. Not the way Gray had refused to back down when her brother had interrupted them in the elevator. So she'd chalked up the step backward to her usual mistake of moving a little fast.

At least he still seemed interested.

He'd eaten lunch with her every day at the café in the Kendall building atrium and had insisted on following her to work in the morning and home at night. He'd even volunteered to make a run to the coffee shop tonight when she told him she needed to work late.

There was still hope.

That wasn't the case with the investigation into who had pushed her into the street. Ash had found nothing. No one who remembered a woman in a powder-blue sweatshirt. No one who noticed the vicious shove. No one who could tell them anything.

At least nothing like that had happened again.

Knuckles wrapped on the open door. Gray poked his head inside. "How's the work coming?"

"I'm craving my drug of choice."

He stepped into the room, two cups from her favorite coffee shop in his fists. "Caffeine, it is. Double shot, low-fat latte." He crossed the room and handed her one of the cups.

The rich scent of espresso perked up her senses. She brought it to her lips and took a long, creamy sip. "Ahh, you're my savior."

"You're staying awfully late."

"I need to get caught up. Rachel needs my help with some wedding details, but the work doesn't wait, you know?"

"Not unless you tell it to wait. You need to do that sometimes, you know. You don't want people to start calling you a workaholic." He gave her a smile and took a sip out of his own cup.

"Me? A workaholic? Nah, that would be my brother." At least it used to be Devin. Since he had asked Jolie to marry him, he'd mellowed and become a little more well-rounded. Jolie had a good influence on him.

He smiled and plopped down in one of the chairs facing her desk. "You can't like hanging out here this late at night. Everyone else has gone home."

It was true. Even Devin had left. "I'm a little nervous. But there's no reason. Being from security, you of all people can see I'm pretty safe here." Of course, the parking ramp would be empty and dark. And even though Devin had ordered increased security and she'd be driving instead of walking, the streets downtown were pretty vacant this time of night. She took another soothing gulp.

"But?"

Funny that she just met him, and yet he seemed to read her mind. She shook her head. "It's not logical."

"Fear often isn't. But that doesn't make it not real."

Where did this guy come from? He couldn't be this perceptive, could he? Could an actual man be this in tune with what she was thinking? Know just what to say and how to say it so she didn't feel like a wimp? She shook her head.

"What now?"

"You're too good to be true."

He looked away, as if expecting someone at the door. No one was there.

Natalie bit the inside of her lower lip. Leave it to her to go too far, say too much. Just like kissing him the day he'd saved her from traffic. Whenever she found a decent man, the one or two in existence, she had a habit of falling too hard, too fast. She couldn't help it. She wished she could skip the games, just get that ring on her finger and know he was always going to be there.

But men never saw it that way. They seemed to want the chase, the hunt. If she gave herself to them too fast, they no longer wanted her.

And that's when they would leave. "I'll be fine."

He unfolded himself from the chair and straightened to his full height. "I'll let you finish what you have to do. I'll be right outside the office catching up on some of my own stuff. Whenever you want to leave, I'm ready."

"You know, your security job doesn't require you to follow the executives home."

"This has nothing to do with the job. Don't you know that yet?" He gave her a smile that made her bones feel soft. "Unless you want me to install an alarm system at your place while I'm there."

She let out a laugh. It felt good. Normal. And she had to admit, she was glad he was willing to stay until she was finished with this project. She had been dreading the trip home without his reassuring headlights shining behind her more than she wanted to admit. "Can you give me about two hours?"

He didn't hesitate. "No problem."

She still felt guilty. Two hours was a long time to sit around and wait. She was probably pushing it. "You sure you don't mind?"

He held her gaze, his hazel eyes clear and sincere. "I'm sure. And the next time you ask, I'll still be sure."

Warmth spread over her skin. Her knees felt a little wobbly. Crazy. Flushing. Weak knees. She was turning into a cliché. The next thing she knew, she'd be picking out a song for their wedding and he'd be running for the hills.

"I'll meet you at the elevator in exactly two hours."

He gave her a nod, not breaking eye contact for a second. "Two hours it is."

He took his coffee out into the hall and closed the door behind him.

By the time she'd gotten herself composed, almost ten minutes had passed, and she had to work as fast as she could to accomplish all she needed to by the two-hour deadline she'd set.

He was waiting for her at the elevator as promised.

She'd never known a guy this considerate, let alone dated one, if one lunch and one kiss and a lot of following her in his car could be considered dating. Here she'd just met him, and yet he made her feel so cared for, so safe, she wanted him to put a ring on her finger right now, recite the vows and be done with it.

God, she was pitiful. Give her a double shot, low-fat latte, and she'll promise her life.

Maybe Jolie was right, in a way. But instead of it being Gray who couldn't be trusted, it was Natalie herself.

She took a gulp of coffee and willed the caffeine to clear her mind and bring her back to reality. Unless she wanted to chase him off, she'd better watch it.

She behaved like a perfect lady, yet as they rode down to the parking garage, got in their cars and he followed her through the dark streets to Hortense Place, all she could think of was how hard she could fall for this guy. How much she wanted to kiss him again.

And how much she wanted more than that.

She turned into the long driveway and passed through the gate. The grounds were quiet, only a single light gleaming from the mansion's first floor. She wound past the pool house and through the gardens. She pulled up in front of the little garage. Lights flicked on. For a second, her heart jolted, then she remembered the motion sensing lights her uncle had promised to have installed.

She hit the button on her remote, and the garage door rose. But instead of driving inside, she pushed open the door and stepped out into the drive.

She had to be out of her mind, doing this. But she couldn't resist. This tension between her and Gray either had to lead to another kiss, or she had to put the friend label on him and make sure it stuck. This not knowing if there was something between them was driving her crazy.

A tremor seized low in her belly. She forced her feet to carry her to his car.

When she arrived, he already had the door open and was uncurling his body from behind the wheel. "Is something wrong?"

"Ahh, no."

"Then what is it? The garage door not working or something."

"No. I was just wondering…" She swallowed into a parched throat. She couldn't go on. She had no idea what to say.

"You're going to show me your paintings?"

The request caught her off guard. She'd totally forgotten he wanted to see her paintings. Paintings she hadn't purposely shown anyone except Ash the night of the break-in. Paintings which would not make him interested in her, but likely have the opposite effect.

To her horror, she found herself nodding.

"Great." Gray reached into his car and shut off the ignition. He slammed the door and turned to look at her.

Her paintings. A quiver started in her chest and moved through her whole body. Could she really show Gray something that personal? Something that raw?

What had she gotten herself into?

NATALIE STARED AT HIM as if shell-shocked.

He narrowed his eyes on her. He'd tossed out the idea of seeing her paintings because he wanted a look at them. Obviously that was not what Natalie had in mind. He reached out and laid a hand on her arm. "Are you okay?"

"Um, yeah. Come on in." She waved an arm, motioning for him to follow her into the garage.

He didn't budge. "You don't really want to show me your paintings, do you?"

She chewed on her bottom lip. Her fingers flexed at her sides, her fists opening and closing.

Obviously her paintings were very personal. He felt guilty for pushing. "I understand."

She met his eyes, as if looking for something.

He gave her what he hoped was an understanding smile. Natalie might not be considered a classic beauty by some people, but he found her more attractive than any movie star he'd ever seen. There was something about her that riveted him. She had such a joy for life, yet underneath he sensed a sadness he wanted to soothe. Standing here right now, it was all he could do to keep from kissing her. No, not just that. He wanted to make love to her and know everything about her. He wanted to hold her and make her his.

"No, it's okay. I'll show you."

"You sure?"

She nodded. "I want to." She led him into the little house.

The cottage was light and airy inside, just as he expected. Hardwood floors stretched through the kitchen and dinette. Light marble countertops and bright splashes of color here and there looked cheery, yet soft. The living area featured neutral carpet, a fireplace and a light leather couch that looked comfortable enough to melt into. Natalie turned into a hallway. She passed a bathroom and stopped at what looked like a bedroom door.

"This is it?"

She glanced back at him. Pushing the door open, she stepped back. "This is it."

He stepped onto the smooth tile floor, Natalie right behind him. The space was a good size for what was originally a bedroom, but it was jammed with half a dozen easels, four of which had partially shredded canvases propped on them. Other painting supplies, including more canvas, filled a series of shelves and other storage stretching along two walls. "Looks like you have a nice setup here."

"My aunt and uncle insisted. I don't think they really wanted me to move out of the big house. But since I did, they wanted the guest cottage to have everything I needed."

"Nice." He crossed the room to get a better look at the easels. Natalie followed, her heels clicking on the floor. He scanned each canvas, piecing together shreds where he had to, hyperaware of her watching him.

All the paintings had a similar theme. Shadows. The dark figure of a man. And on each, pools of red that looked like blood. Some of the images were at a distance. Some close-up. But whatever the perspective, all had an ominous feel. A shiver clawed at the back of Gray's neck.

"You don't like them."

He shook his head. "It's not that. They're just so dark. I didn't expect that from you."

"I told you they aren't exactly commercial. I paint my nightmares."

Those had to be some awful dreams. He focused on what appeared to be blood spatters covering a shadowy close-up of a man's face. "Nightmares about what?"

She shifted her shoes on the tile. "Just nightmares. I paint them to get them out of my head. I try not to dwell on them."

In other words, she didn't want to tell him. He couldn't blame her. They hadn't known each other that long, at least she hadn't known him. He'd been watching her so closely the past weeks, he had the sense that he knew her. Obviously what he knew only scratched the surface. "Do you only paint nightmares?"

"I don't have a lot of time to paint now that I'm working so much at Kendall Communications. But I used to paint flowers in the shade garden and frost on the evergreens." She gestured to the panel of windows peering out into dark gardens. "Those subjects were a lot more commercial. I sold quite a few paintings back then."

From the corner of his eye, he spotted something shifting in the shadows outside. Bigger than an animal, too substantial for a swaying tree branch.

"Do you want to stay a little while? I have wine. We could build a fire."

He focused on the spot where he'd seen movement. Too late. The gardens and the cove of evergreens beyond stood perfectly still. Beyond that, it was too dark to see.

"Or not. It's kind of late, and I'm sure you are busy tomorrow."

"No." He grasped her hand. Truth was, he'd love to spend some time with her all cozy in this cottage of hers. He'd been thinking about it all week. Dreaming about it. He must have taken five extra showers in the past few days, all of them cold. "I think it's a great—"

There it was again.

Gray didn't want to pull his eyes from Natalie's. Not now. Not when he knew she'd read it the wrong way the first time. But there was no helping it. He could swear something was moving out there.

He turned away from her and looked out the window. He'd only gotten the slightest glimpse, but he could swear the darkness shifted. Moved.

There it was again.

His gut tightened. Devin hadn't mentioned anything about the police staking out Natalie's cabin. That left only one likely explanation. Someone was out there. Watching. Waiting for him to leave. Biding his time until Natalie was alone. Vulnerable.

He'd never let it happen.

Even though the lights were somewhat dim inside Natalie's studio, they were still bright enough to give him more reflection than night vision through the glass. He needed to get out there, find out who was watching. "I really have to go."

"Oh. Okay."

He recognized the hurt in her voice. No doubt she thought he was rejecting her. A misperception that would make him laugh if the situation wasn't so serious. "I'll see you tomorrow?"

"Of course. We work in the same building."

"I'll meet you here. We can drive in together."

She narrowed her eyes, as if trying to figure out what was behind the offer. "That's not necessary."

"I want to."

"You don't want to stay tonight, but you want to drive all the way up here just so you can follow my car?"

Little did she know he didn't plan to go anywhere tonight. "I would like to stay. I just…can't."

She nodded, a resigned look on her face. "I'll see you at work."

He wanted to explain. Not tell her the truth. He'd promised Devin he wouldn't do that. But the idea of her believing he didn't want her...

She walked him to the door. Standing to the side, she crossed her arms over her chest.

"I'll be here tomorrow morning." Without waiting for another protest, he opened the door and stepped into the night. She shut it behind him, and he could hear her slide the dead bolt into place.

He walked to his car and slid behind the wheel, before turning back to check on the house. The foyer light clicked off.

Natalie giving up on him.

He should ease out of the drive, park on a side street and return on foot to surprise whoever was hiding in the gardens. With Natalie as bait, he could stalk the stalker, get the drop on him.

Instead he pulled out his cell phone and called up a number.

"Yes?" Devin Kendall answered in a clipped voice.

"Grayson Scott. Do the cops have someone outside Natalie's?"

"They said they couldn't. Not enough manpower, and she hasn't been attacked. The best they would do was take a drive by every hour or two."

That's what he'd suspected. If the Kendalls

weren't loaded and brother Ash wasn't a cop himself, Gray doubted the locals would have been able to do that much in light of recent budget cuts.

So it wasn't a cop. That made his choices clear. "Thanks."

"What's going on?"

"I think someone might be watching Natalie's house."

"Gray, you'd better—"

"Natalie's safety is my only priority. She'll be fine, I guarantee. But you might want to ask that cop to stop by five minutes ago. And tell your aunt and uncle to lock their doors." He disconnected the call. Setting the ring to mute, he returned it to his pocket, pulled out his Glock and climbed from the car.

He kept close to the evergreen trees rimming the garden. It was cold again tonight, unseasonably cold for November in St. Louis. His breath fogged in the air. With each step, he could feel the grass—stiff with frost—crunch slightly before giving beneath the sole of his shoe.

When he reached the area where he thought he'd spotted movement, he paused, willing his eyes to see in the tree-filtered moonlight. Sure enough. The frost-touched grass bowed, flattened to the ground.

The prints were smaller than his, but considering he wore a size twelve, that wasn't saying much. He traced their path, circling the garden's edge, flanking the house. Reaching an expanse of bare earth, he stopped to study a print on the edge.

And noticed something shining in the moonlight.

Nails. The four-inch spikes littered the mulch under a set of windows. What the hell?

He pulled out his phone.

Devin answered on the first ring. "Yeah?"

"Has Natalie had any carpentry work done recently?"

"No, why?"

He filled Devin in on what he'd found. "In light of everything that's happened, I'd like to get Natalie out of here until your brother and the cops can check out what's going on."

"Good idea."

"Your aunt and uncle, too."

"Leave them to me. I'm on my way right now. Ash is, too." He cut off the call.

Gray circled the cottage and headed straight to the main entrance. Natalie's safety had to be his priority. As much as he wanted to catch this guy, that wasn't why he was here. Luckily Devin saw things his way and didn't hesitate to respond.

He made it back to the front door in seconds and hit the bell. A few more seconds and the soft footfalls of bare feet sounded on the other side.

Natalie pulled the door open and stared at him from under lowered eyebrows. Her long blond hair was pulled back from her face. Her bathrobe dipped in a deep V between her breasts and cinched tight around her narrow waist. "I thought—"

"Come with me."

"What?"

He took a breath. The damn footprint and nails had him so shaken, he'd forgotten she didn't know he was here to protect her. "Screw my early morning."

Her eyebrows shot upward.

"You showed me your place. I want to show you mine."

Chapter Seven

Natalie didn't know what she expected Gray's apartment to look like, but it sure wasn't this. She scanned the Spartan room. White walls stretched from corner to corner, unbroken except by windows. The beige carpet seemed brand-new, and she doubted the stove had ever been used. "Did you just move in?"

"I suppose it looks pretty empty to you."

Empty, yes. But not the clichéd bachelor kind of empty. Except for a jacket draped on a kitchen chair and two pairs of shoes tossed carelessly to the side of the door, the place looked cleaner than her house.

And it was far from being a hovel. One look out the window and the sparkling lights of the city made one forget there was no art on the walls. And though little more than a leather couch broke up the living space, it was a piece anyone would be proud to own.

Gray seemed to have good taste and money. "You don't spend much time at home?"

"No, not much."

She knew she was prying, but she couldn't help it. She liked Gray. A lot. He'd seen her paintings, and now she wanted to know everything about him, even though he seemed about as eager to share as she had been.

She could just imagine what Jolie would say about that.

Pushing her friend's concerned warnings to the back of her mind, Natalie stepped to the window and peered outside. Jolie was probably right to worry and not just about Natalie's growing crush on a man she barely knew.

Something had been going on at the mansion tonight, something no one seemed to want to tell her about. She noticed Ash's car in the drive on their way out, and she could swear they passed Devin just a few blocks into the drive to Gray's. She called Ash on the cell, but while he'd admitted he was talking to Aunt Angela and Uncle Craig, he'd revealed little else. She had to wonder if they'd learned something.

Maybe something about whoever murdered their parents all those years ago.

She could feel Gray move up behind her.

For a second, she could imagine him putting his arms around her and pulling her back against his chest. Warm, safe, protected. The sensation was so vivid, she let out a sigh.

"What is it?"

"Nothing." She had the urge to tell him what she'd been imagining, then discarded the idea. She really liked Gray, and one of the things she ought to have learned about men by now was she couldn't lay too much on them too quickly.

"Sure? You seem worried."

Too much too quickly included trauma and craziness. Considering the amount of each that had entered her life since Gray and she met, she'd probably reached her quota. "Not worried. Just looking out at the view."

"Afraid of heights?"

"Maybe a little. Especially when I look up." She craned her neck to take in the taller building visible at the side of the window. "But it is a stunning view."

"For a lower floor, it's not too shabby. That's the reason I rented the place." His voice rumbled close to her ear, but he didn't touch her.

She fought the urge to lean back against him. She couldn't figure it out. When he'd left her house, she assumed he wasn't interested. But then he'd returned and asked her to come to his apartment. And seeing that he'd refused her when she'd asked him to stay at her house, she'd better let him take the lead this time. Play a little hard to get.

A good idea…in theory. Too bad she was terrible when it came to playing love games. It always seemed dishonest to her. Her aunt always said she wore her heart on her sleeve. It sure made it easy to break, but she'd never figured out how to do things differently.

No wonder she was still alone.

She wrapped her arms around her middle.

"Cold?"

She gave a shrug, not wanting to tell him where the need to hold herself had really come from. "A little, I guess."

"Just a second." He turned away from her and walked down the short hall that must have led to the bedrooms. When he returned, he was carrying a dark colored blanket. He draped it around her shoulders.

Not what she had in mind, but she gathered the blanket tight anyway. It was prickly, probably made of wool. The kind of blanket that could get wet and wouldn't lose its insulating properties. "Is this a military blanket?"

"Except for the comforter on the bed, it's all I have. Sorry."

"You were in the army?"

A muscle along his jaw flexed and he peered past her and out the window. "Navy."

"So you served on a ship?" Funny, she didn't see him as the sailor type. Not at all.

"I was in special forces."

A little shiver ran through her. "A SEAL?"

He gave his head an almost imperceptible nod.

She always thought of Navy SEALs as being brash, larger than life. But while Gray was strong and had a forceful aura about him, he seemed more quiet and self-reflective. He did have the sex appeal she'd expect, though. Plenty of that. "Did you like being a SEAL?"

"It was the best time of my life."

"Why aren't you still serving?"

The muscle along his jaw twitched and tightened. Again he looked out at the lights as if he didn't want her to see what was in his eyes. "I was injured."

"Oh, my God, what happened?"

"You heard about the USS *Cole?*"

Of course she had. It had happened a long time ago, and she hadn't been old enough to really pay attention to the details. "It was bombed, right?"

He nodded. "By a small group of terrorists

in a raft. They weren't seen as a threat and got close enough to damage the ship."

She remembered. "And people died. Sailors on the ship."

"Yes." He took a deep breath, the inhalation rough enough to be a shudder. "That wasn't the only attempt of that kind on a navy ship."

"Another ship was bombed?"

"No. Thank God, the terrorists weren't successful. At least we were able to keep that from happening."

"We? Meaning your SEAL team? You stopped a terrorist attack?" Maybe the news should have come as a surprise, but although she hadn't heard about any other ships being attacked, she wasn't surprised Gray had been able to thwart terrorists. After the way he'd scooped her out of busy traffic, she'd probably believe he was a superhero without too much difficulty. "That's amazing. You're amazing."

He shook his head. His brows hunkered low over his eyes. "No, I'm not amazing."

"I don't understand."

"The operation didn't go as planned."

"And that's how you got hurt." What was wrong with her? Why hadn't she put that together before? "What happened?"

He waited a long time before he spoke again. "We stopped the raft before it got close enough to damage the ship, but the ordnance was on a timer."

"It went off?"

He nodded.

"You're lucky you weren't killed."

That faraway look again. As if he was peering back at a past he didn't want to acknowledge, didn't want to remember. As if he felt somehow responsible.

She knew that look. She still saw it in the mirror some days. "Somebody *was* killed."

He didn't move. He didn't answer.

He didn't have to. She knew she was right. Even without knowing the details, she wanted to tell him it wasn't his fault. Maybe because she'd heard those words so many times when she was young. But words like that didn't do any good. At least she'd never believed them. Still didn't. "Who?"

"Best SEAL I ever knew. And a good friend. We grew up together right here in St. Louis."

"Oh, my God, I'm so sorry."

He turned his head to look at her for the first time since she'd asked about the blanket. "It should have been me."

"Oh, Gray, no." Natalie covered his lips with her fingertips. "You can't say that."

He didn't speak, but she could see by the sadness in his eyes that no matter what she thought about his statement, he wasn't about to change his mind.

That didn't mean she wasn't going to try. "I know how you feel, but you can't let yourself think that. You can't go there."

He didn't move. For a moment she wasn't sure if he was listening to her or had faded off once again to that faraway place.

She moved her hand from his mouth and smoothed it over his cheek, razor stubble prickling her fingers. She cradled his jaw beneath his ear. She didn't know what to say to make him listen, but she knew what she could do to show him how she felt. Rising onto her tiptoes, she covered his lips with hers.

Her kiss was tentative at first. Gentle. Sweet. She wanted more than anything for him to know she cared. That she wanted to take away his pain, even though she knew she never could. She kissed his upper lip, then his lower, each a whisper of a touch. She looked into his eyes.

He returned her gaze. Not faraway now, his eyes delved into hers. He brought his arms up her sides and around her waist. He pulled her body against the length of his and claimed her mouth.

This kiss was far from sweet, far from gentle. She'd never felt anything so urgent before, on the edge of control. She wanted to let loose. To taste him, feel him, have him for her own. She circled his neck with her arms and stretched tall to press the length of her body against him. Her senses melded together, the scent of his body, of his leather jacket, the cinnamon fragrance of the room. The scent of her own perfume. The roughness of stubble on his chin and solid muscle of his chest.

Before she realized what she was doing, she found the buttons of his shirt. She fought them open with shaking fingers. She pulled his shirttail from his pants and slipped her hands inside. Her fingers skimmed over smooth skin and hard muscle. She closed her eyes and just felt.

He hesitated, then drew back from the kiss. "We can't do this."

She opened her eyes and looked into his. "It's okay."

"I'm sure your brother wouldn't agree."

She smiled up at Gray and shook her head.

"If you hadn't noticed before, my brothers are a little overprotective."

"They care about you."

"They do. But that doesn't mean they know what is best for me." Or even if they did, she didn't care. Right now all she could think about was how much she wanted Gray. She knew she was too impulsive, too eager to give her heart, too quick to throw herself over the cliff. But that didn't change anything. It was who she was. And no matter what Devin said and Jolie said and anyone else said, she knew Gray was different. She could feel it every moment they were together.

She unbuttoned her blouse and let the silk slide down her arms. She wasn't sure why she'd worn her black lace bra today. She'd thought of Gray when she'd put it on this morning. Fantasized about him seeing her in it, her breasts full, her nipples straining against the delicate fabric. The lace's light floral pattern concealed nothing, and as the blouse fell to the floor, she felt a thrill at being so exposed.

His gaze ran over her.

Her skin felt electric, as if he was touching her with his hands. Her nipples hardened and pressed against the lace. She wanted more than his eyes on her; she wanted to feel his rough palms, the warm wetness of his mouth. She wanted his heat pressed against her, wrapped around her, inside her.

She stepped toward him and reached for his hands. She placed his palms over the lace cups and molded them to her.

He smiled. "You are something."

She returned the smile, feeling emboldened by his tone of voice. "I hope you mean that in a good way."

"I mean it in a great way." He moved his palms against her. He lowered his head and took one nipple into his mouth. He caressed her and kissed her until she couldn't take it anymore. If she didn't have him now, she thought she might scream.

Pulling away from him, she slipped the bra's straps down her arms. She was taking a risk, but after making the leap of showing him her paintings, this felt easy. Natural. And the way he was looking at her made her feel she could do anything and Gray would be there for her anyway. She hadn't known him long, and yet she felt as if she knew him better than anyone she'd ever dated.

And she wanted to know him every way she could.

She arched her back and unhooked her bra, letting her breasts spill free. She threw the bra to the side then slipped off her trousers. Wearing only a thong, she climbed up on Gray's bed.

Moonlight streamed through the bank of windows and bathed her skin in its blue glow. She stretched out on the bed and turned to Gray, wanting to feel him beside her. He hadn't moved, not one muscle but his eyes. Those sexy eyes. They reached out to her, hunger plain on his face, and right then she felt like she was the sexiest and strongest and most secure woman on the planet.

GRAY COULD HARDLY BELIEVE he was there, watching Natalie climb on his bed, the moonlight caressing her body, her breasts. He shouldn't be doing this, shouldn't be taking advantage of her this way. She didn't know who he was, not really. Didn't know her brother had hired him as her bodyguard. She deserved to know.

But how could he walk away from a dream?

His fingers found his belt and unbuckled it. He might regret this later, but now he couldn't think that far ahead. He wouldn't let himself.

He had just stripped his pants and was about to divest himself of his briefs when he noticed it. A spot of red. It skipped over the bed and skimmed Natalie's flat belly and centered right above her perfect left breast.

Realization clicked into place. What he was seeing. What it meant. His breath froze in his chest.

Oh, God, no.

He sprang onto the bed. He felt like he was moving too slow, too awkwardly. He grabbed Natalie's ankle, his fingers closing around her smooth skin, holding her tight. He yanked her toward him with all his strength.

Her mouth rounded into an O. A shocked cry escaped her lips. She slid over the comforter, away from the window, out from under that deadly red beam.

When she reached the edge of the bed, he bent down and scooped her into his arms. He had no time to lose. He shifted his weight, wanting to dash clear, knowing he could never move quickly enough.

The window exploded. Glass rained across the bed.

Natalie screamed.

Gray clamped her tight to his chest and ran.

Chapter Eight

A second shot smashed through the glass and hit the bed. The next pinged off the floor a few feet away.

Adrenaline pounded through Gray's body, sharpening detail, making everything feel as if it was moving in slow motion.

Especially him.

He had to move faster. He had to reach cover. He had to ensure Natalie's safety.

He reached the master bath and dashed inside. His feet slapped cold tile. He slipped and went down to a knee. The force shuddered up his bad leg, but he hardly noticed.

"Natalie. Please say you're okay. You have to be okay." He brushed his fingers over the silk of her hair. His hand trembled.

"I'm okay. I'm okay." Her voice sounded as shaky as he felt, but it was the sweetest sound he'd ever heard.

"Thank God." He pulled in breath after

shuddering breath. For someone who had seen combat, he felt like he'd just gotten out of basic. He was a shaking, out-of-control mess. They were out of the line of fire. His next step had to be getting control of himself.

He concentrated on slowing his breathing. He laid Natalie gently on the bathroom rug.

She sat cross-legged and braced herself with her hands. She was nearly naked, but she didn't move to cover herself. She simply stared at him with wild eyes. "What was that?"

He scanned her body, looking for injuries. "Are you hit?"

"Hit? You mean, shot? Someone was shooting at us?"

"Yes. Are you hurt?" The flesh that had been so sexy just moments before now seemed incredibly fragile to him, precious. He'd never forgive himself if she was hurt.

"I'm okay. How would somebody be shooting?"

He continued to look her over. He couldn't see any blood, but he needed to make sure. A lot of glass had been flying. As frightened as she was, she could be cut and not even notice.

"Oh, my God, you're hurt." Natalie pointed out a trail of blood on his arm, not much more than a scratch.

"It's nothing."

She pulled her legs up and huddled forward, as if she'd recovered from the shock enough to feel the need to cover her bare breasts. "Now what do we do? My phone is out in my bag. We need to call the police."

Gray thrust to his feet. He grabbed his robe from a hook near the shower and gave it to her. "Put this on."

Remaining seated, she pulled the robe over her body and tied it snug at the waist. She wrapped her arms across her chest as if cold.

He ran a hand down her arm. "Now you're going to stay here. I'll take care of this."

"The gunman could be still out there."

"I know. I'll be careful."

At first she looked like she might argue, then she dropped her gaze to the floor and gave a weak nod.

He hated to see her like this. When she was on his bed, she looked beautiful, powerful, brash. Now she seemed smaller, and the thought of that transformation being his fault dug deep.

He never should have brought her to his apartment, to his bed. He knew why he'd done it. It was obvious, after all. After her invitation back at her cottage, he'd known what she was thinking. And instead of checking her into a hotel and standing sentry outside her door, he'd brought her here so he could sleep with her.

He'd been self-centered and way out of line. And then what had he done? He hadn't bothered to take a glance at the building next door. He hadn't drawn the blinds. He'd stood there and admired how the moonlight showed off Natalie's breasts.

He really was as selfish as Sherry had said.

Patting her hand a final time, he forced himself to step away and slipped out of the bathroom. He moved quickly, his breathing regular and controlled, his heartbeat steady as spring rain. Now that he was alone and didn't have to worry about Natalie getting hit, he felt like he was back in his own skin. He'd spent years training for combat, and he was damn good at it.

Using furniture as cover, he went for the closet first. There he slipped on a pair of sweatpants and some sneakers, grabbed a weapon from his gun safe and jammed a loaded clip into place. If the sniper was still in the neighboring building, he'd be dead before he could squeeze off another round.

He went for his pants next and the cell phone strapped to his belt. Glass shards crunched under his rubber soles. Wind whistled through the shattered pane. He eyed the windows and followed the trajectory to the neighboring building. No figure in any of the possible windows. No movement. The guy had probably been smart enough to clear out. The gunshots had been loud. They would have been noticed. Likely the police were already on their way.

The faint sound of sirens screamed above the howling of wind through the window, as if answering his thought.

He shook the glass from his pants and retrieved his cell phone. Locating Natalie's clothing, he shook out glass. She couldn't wear them like this. He'd have to find something else for her to put on. Something that would broadcast to the world why he'd taken her back to his apartment and what they'd been doing when the bullets had started to fly. By the time this was over, he'd be lucky he had a job, but the thing he really regretted was never again seeing the confident gleam in Natalie's eyes that she'd had lying in the middle of his bed.

After this, he'd be lucky if she wanted to look at him at all.

NATALIE CROSSED HER ARMS over her chest and tried to pretend that every cop in the place couldn't see that she was braless under Gray's oversize T-shirt. She still felt as shaky and out of breath as when the glass had shattered over her head, but now she could add a touch of nausea to the mix. At least Devin hadn't commented when he saw her wearing Gray's things. Neither had Ash, a miracle in itself. But she knew it wasn't because they hadn't noticed.

Ash finished talking to an evidence tech and motioned Natalie into the hall. As soon as he closed the door, he wrapped her in a hug. "Thank God you're okay."

She pressed her head against his shoulder and willed herself not to cry. As much as she bemoaned her family's hovering, she always knew they cared about her. And that they would be there for her whenever she needed them.

And that was the best feeling in the world.

Ash ended the hug. He held her upper arms and studied her eyes. "Do you remember a guy named Timothy Walters?"

She knew the name. She searched her memory. "He used to work for Kendall, right?"

"He was in your department."

"I remember." Her stomach felt even more unstable at the memory. A clean-cut guy with a short temper and a habit of snapping at clients. "I had to fire him."

Ash nodded. "Seems he was upset about it, too. Upset enough to send you threatening letters to the office and your place."

"I never got any letters."

"Uncle Craig didn't want you to see them. Neither did Devin."

Now her uncle was throwing in with her brothers, too? She pulled in a deep breath. Not that she could say she would have welcomed the letters. Firing the man had been stressful enough. "So what does that mean? I fired him a couple of years ago."

"Yes, but I want to talk to him anyway. Sometimes the resentments build up only to explode much later. Our family has been in the news. Something like that could have set him off."

She nodded. It didn't make a lot of sense to her, but she had read stories in the paper and seen plenty of dramas on television where just such circumstances led to murderous sprees. But even though she knew it was possible, the thought that *she* would be in the middle of circumstances like that seemed unreal.

"There's another possible trigger, too," Ash continued. "I talked to his wife. She just split with him the day before your cottage was vandalized."

A shiver fanned up her spine. "So he split up with his wife, and he blames me in some strange way?"

"I don't know. We have an APB out on him. We'll find him, and we'll find the truth." He gave her another quick hug. "Don't worry."

She'd been nearly shot and might be the target of a sick mind holding resentments. What was to worry about?

She offered Ash her best confident smile. "I'll be fine."

The fact that Ash was on the case and making progress should make her feel better. But her hands still shook, and her knees still felt like they'd buckle at any moment. Even hovered over by her brothers and standing in an apartment crawling with cops, she didn't feel safe. "Where is Gray?"

"In the kitchen with Devin. I don't know if you want to go in there, though."

"Why not?"

"You know how Devin gets when it comes to protecting family."

Great, so her older brother hadn't said a word to her about being in Gray's bedroom when the shooting started, because he was saving it all for Gray. She eyed Ash. "Yeah, I know how he gets, as if you're any better."

Ash shrugged. "Devin gets first crack at him. I'm next. Gray is just lucky Thad isn't here. Then he'd have to explain himself three times."

"Ash, I don't need my brothers to be breathing down the neck of every guy I date. I can make my own decisions."

He gave her a raised-brow look that answered for him.

Arguing was no use. She turned away from Ash and started for the kitchen.

"Good luck, Natalie," Ash called after her.

Natalie stopped outside the arched entrance to the kitchen and listened for a second. It didn't take more than that for Devin's voice to reach her.

"I told you to take her somewhere safe, not take her to bed." Her oldest brother was in full-on protective mode, as Ash had warned. She hadn't heard him so angry in a long while.

"My building is security locked and has a doorman. It's the safest place I know," Gray said. "I didn't intend for the rest to happen."

Devin scoffed. "So while Ash and I were busy checking the cottage and mansion grounds, you thought you'd take advantage."

Buzzing rose in Natalie's ears. She'd been with Gray since they left the Kendall offices. When had he talked to Devin? Her breath caught in her throat. There had been those moments after she'd asked him to stay and before he'd invited her to his place. Had Gray spent that time calling her brother? Why on earth would he do that?

"It wasn't like that."

No, it wasn't. If anyone was taking advantage and pushing for sex, it had been her. And she didn't feel a bit sorry about it.

She'd wanted to make love with Gray. She'd more than wanted it; she'd done her best to make it happen. And despite the gunshots, she wanted it to happen again. She finally found a guy who was different. Who she really liked and who seemed to like her in return. Maybe enough for it to lead somewhere. And now her brother's overprotective bullying—

"Devin, it won't happen again."

A leaden weight settled into Natalie's stomach.

"You're damn right it's not going to happen again. Because as soon as I arrange for a replacement tomorrow, you're fired."

Natalie gasped out loud. She couldn't believe what she'd just heard. She whirled around the doorjamb and glared at her brother, her fists balled by her sides. "How dare you, Devin? You can't fire him. He deserves to have a private life, too. You might be able to lay down the rules at the office, but you can't dictate what employees do on their own time."

Devin's eyebrows pulled together.

Gray stepped toward Natalie before her brother had a chance to speak. "It's okay, Natalie. He's right. I never should have brought you here."

If she thought she felt nauseated before, she'd been wrong. She wrapped her arms around her stomach. She knew that tone of voice. The tone that led up to *it's not you, it's me.* Or *it's just not a good time in my life right now.* Or *the boss says I should back off and I don't like you enough to disagree.* "What are you saying?"

Gray looked at her, his lips half-open, but no words came out. Instead, it was Devin who spoke. "Grayson isn't on his own time, Natalie. This is his job, being with you, keeping you safe. I'm sorry I didn't tell you, but I knew you'd argue, say I was hovering. But after tonight, I think we can agree the steps I took were warranted."

Natalie couldn't breathe. She could see

the pieces of the puzzle displayed in front of her, but her mind resisted shuffling them into place. Or maybe it was her heart.

She looked from her brother to Gray. "I don't understand."

Gray met her gaze, his expression a mix of regret and defeat. "I work for your brother, Natalie. But I'm not an alarm system expert. I'm your bodyguard."

GRAY WATCHED THE LOOK in Natalie's eyes go from confusion to betrayal.

"Why didn't you tell me? Did Ash know about this, too?"

"Natalie," Devin said, as he stepped toward his sister and took hold of her arm.

She ripped away from his grasp. "I don't want to talk to you, Devin. Ash, either. This doesn't even surprise me about the two of you."

Gray stepped toward her. Devin was far from his favorite person at the moment, and he should have been honest with Natalie at the first about hiring a bodyguard. But even so, the last thing Gray wanted was for Natalie to blame her brother. All that would do is drive a wedge in the Kendall family and cause Natalie and her brothers more pain. "Natalie, there's a real danger out there. You can't deny it. Devin was only trying to keep you safe."

Natalie spun around and glared at him as if he'd just slapped her. "Devin, will you leave us?"

Devin didn't budge. "I think we should talk this out."

She spoke to her brother without sparing him a glance. "So you can say what? Someone is trying to kill me and you were protecting me. I get that. Someone just shot at me. I'm not trying to deny I'm in danger any longer. What I don't get is why you didn't tell me the truth."

"I did tell you I was worried for your life after all that happened to Ash and me since Rick Campbell was exonerated. You said I was overreacting. You said you didn't want a bodyguard hovering over you."

She still didn't look at her brother, her gaze riveted on Gray. "I did say that, and you should have listened to me. Or at least talked about it again after my cottage was vandalized and I was pushed into the street. But you didn't have to revisit the subject, did you? Because I already had a bodyguard."

In his peripheral vision, Gray could see Devin glance from Natalie to him. He'd do anything to fix this rift, to say the magic words that would make this go away, to go back in time and tell her the truth that first night in the parking garage, anything. Obviously his options were much more limited. Still, he had to find some way for this to work out. For Natalie and her brothers and for him.

Natalie raised her chin and let out a shaky breath. "Now please leave us alone, Devin. I need to talk to Gray."

"Okay, okay. We can talk more later." Devin strode from the room and closed the door behind him.

For a long while, neither Gray nor Natalie spoke. Low voices filtered in from the room next door. The clock in the corner chimed the hour.

Gray's pulse thumped in his ear. After the shooting tonight, he'd expected Devin to fire him. He'd made peace with that. But he'd hoped Natalie would never have to know about his official role.

It wasn't the job. In the past days, he'd ceased to care about that. Now all he cared about was Natalie. About her relationship with her family. About keeping her safe. But it was more than that, too. And he couldn't deny some of his concern was selfish.

Natalie spoke first. "You lied to me."

What could he say? He had. Straight to her face. "I'm sorry."

"Why didn't you tell me you were my bodyguard? Why didn't you tell me in the parking garage that night?"

"Devin didn't want you to know."

"I know that. I'm asking about you. Why didn't you tell me the truth? Why did you worm your way into my life and make me care about you?"

He'd made a mistake not coming clean with her from their first face-to-face meeting. He needed to come clean with her now. "You were never supposed to know I was following you. But when I saw that guy follow you into the garage, I thought there might be something to it. And by the time I caught up to him, he was already talking to you."

"What do you mean? How long ago did Devin hire you?"

"He called shortly after Campbell was exonerated for your parents' murders and the trouble began."

"You've been following me for weeks."

"Yes."

She opened her mouth, to ask something, to yell at him, to tell him she never wanted to see his face again—he didn't know. She closed it again without speaking.

"It was all about keeping you safe, Natalie."

She turned around. "Really? Was that what it was all about? Because I thought we liked each other. I thought we were dating. But then, stupid me, I also thought you were a Good Samaritan I happened to meet by chance." Her eyes glistened and her lashes spiked with tears. She tilted her head back as if to keep them from brimming over and running down her cheeks. "I am the worst judge of men ever."

"No, you're not. I lied to you. You couldn't have known—"

"That's the point. I never know. I always see what I want to see. With you, I saw someone different. Someone who cared about me. Someone who made me feel secure and strong and good about myself."

"I am those things. I want to be."

She shook her head and let out a bitter laugh. "You were paid to make me feel secure. I'll give you that. But the rest?"

"I do care about you, Natalie."

"Give me a break. If you really cared, you would have told me the truth about who you are. You wouldn't have been able to lie and then sleep with me."

She was right. He'd cared for her, but not

enough to tell her the truth. Not enough to bring her to a hotel and sit outside her door. He'd brought her home because he'd wanted what had unfolded in his bedroom. And he'd been willing to keep up the lie in order to take it.

To take her.

At Jimbo's funeral, his wife had called him self-centered. No one had ever been more right. Even when he wasn't conscious of it, Gray made sure he got what he wanted. No matter who it hurt. No matter who died.

It was other people who were big enough to make sacrifices. Not him.

If he really wanted to make this easier on Natalie, it was about time he started. "You're right. About all of it. And I want you to know that as asinine as I've been these past couple of days, I do care about you."

She said nothing, and he wasn't surprised. He pushed on. "I will get out of your life, let you move on and find a man who deserves you. I promise I will. But—"

She pulled in a sharp breath.

For a second, he thought she might ask him to stay. But again, she didn't speak. She just waited for him to continue.

"But I can't leave until Devin makes arrangements for another bodyguard to take my place."

"I don't want a bodyguard at all."

"Come on, Natalie. I know how you feel, but you can't deny that you're in danger."

"Maybe someone was trying to shoot you. It's your apartment. Maybe I wasn't the target at all."

"You don't really believe that."

She looked back out the window. Tears wound down her cheeks.

Gray wanted nothing more than to wipe them, but he knew she wouldn't accept his touch. He couldn't blame her.

"Tomorrow, when Devin finds a replacement, I'll leave you alone. You can forget you ever met me."

"I will," she said, but her voice lacked conviction.

He nodded. He hoped she could. Because, although he'd only known her up close and personal for a short while, he was certain it would be impossible for him to ever forget her.

Chapter Nine

Natalie stared at her face in the mirror behind the bakery's showcase. Her cheeks were pale, her eyes red and puffy, and despite an almost insane love of cake and frosting and all things wedding, she had no desire to sample any of the amazing creations lined up in front of Rachel, Jolie and her.

Rachel, on the other hand, looked absolutely gorgeous. Although her baby bump was only beginning to round, her face showed all the best signs of motherhood.

In a word, she was glowing.

Natalie had read somewhere that many brides weren't so lucky. Nasty side effects like acne, the redness of rosacea and dry skin were just as common as any kind of attractive glow in the cheeks of a pregnant woman. But not for Rachel. Her skin was creamy, her cheeks holding a delicate flush. Her dark brown hair, pulled back from her face in a half up, half down style, was thick and lustrous. And her hazel eyes glittered as she eyed the cakes. "I have to try the lemon poppy seed and the carrot cake, and I can't pass up something with that chocolate Bavarian crème filling."

The baker, a young energetic woman, smiled. "How about white almond cake, chocolate Bavarian crème filling and whipped crème frosting?"

Jolie moaned and Rachel nodded as fast as her head would move. A second later, the enthusiasm on her face gave way to worry. "The last baker bailed on us without much notice. Our wedding is only a week away. You're sure you can make such a fancy cake so quickly?"

"Not a problem. And we'll guarantee that in writing. If we can't fulfill your wedding dreams, we'll find and pay for someone who will."

Rachel and Jolie exchanged pleased looks.

The baker directed their attention to another batch of little cupcake samples and rattled off possible fillings and frostings, each more decadent than the last. By the time they sat down at a small table with their cake samples, they'd added another half dozen to their tasting plates.

"You're awfully quiet, Natalie," Rachel said as they started to dig in. "Thinking about last night?"

How could she not? "I'm okay."

"Yeah, right," Jolie said. "You're so used to getting shot at that it doesn't even bother you anymore."

Rachel nodded. "You're forgetting who you're talking to, Natalie. All of us have been through some bad stuff lately. We know you're not all right. I don't think any of us are, even now."

Natalie scooped in a deep breath and let it out. "You're right, of course. But that doesn't mean I'm going to let it ruin your wedding preparations. We're sitting here with a table full of cake, for crying out loud."

"We can talk and taste at the same time." Rachel picked up her fork and for a few seconds it was poised over a cupcake-size chocolate-fudge cake with a chocolate-mint filling and whipped cream frosting. "So I'll taste, and you talk."

Jolie picked up her own fork. "And don't forget to dish on Mr. Scott outside."

Natalie resisted the urge to glance out the window where Gray was sitting on a bench, waiting for her to finish cake sampling. Last night she'd been certain that she never wanted to see him again. Today, she was trying her best to stick to that.

Too bad her heart didn't want to cooperate.

She gave her future sisters-in-law a run-down of the shooting, leaving out the fact that she was lying on Gray's bed basically naked when bullets crashed through glass. Even so, when Jolie had asked where they were, Natalie had to admit to being in his bedroom, and judging from the looks they gave her, they didn't need more than that to form a picture in their minds.

"I thought you'd decided you weren't going to get involved with him." Jolie set her fork down and focused a look on Natalie that was more concern than anger.

"I know. I'm sorry I didn't tell you. It was just…" What could she say? How on earth could she possibly explain herself?

Jolie nodded, as if Natalie really didn't have to. "You really like him, don't you?"

Natalie shook her head, but that, too, was a lie. "You were right, Jolie. He wasn't what I thought. Devin hired him to be my body-guard."

Neither Jolie nor Rachel looked surprised.

"You knew?"

"We weren't supposed to tell," Rachel admitted around a bite of white cake with

Frangelico buttercream filling. A spot of frosting dotted her lip. "Ash and Devin thought you'd think they were hovering."

Of course that is what she would have thought. And as last night had proven, she would have been wrong. The danger was plenty real.

Natalie let out a sigh. She picked up a forkful of lemon poppy seed then set it back down without even tasting. "Am I really that difficult to handle?"

"Difficult to handle?" Jolie said, her voice rising with disbelief. "Of course not. You want to be independent, live your own life. That's understandable. And for the record, Devin and Ash *can* be a bit overprotective when it comes to you."

Natalie smiled at her friends. "Thad, too, if he were here. But I don't think it qualifies as overprotective if there is a real danger." The similarity of her words to what Gray had said days ago struck her. He'd been right. Devin and Ash had been right, too. It almost pained her to admit it, but there was no point in denying it now. Someone was after their whole family. She might as well face the facts.

"So what happens now?" Jolie asked.

Natalie could only wish she knew the

answer to that question. "I suppose we'd all better be careful."

"That's a given, Natalie, and not what I was asking about." She nodded her head in Gray's direction. "It's obvious that you really like him."

Thickness filled her throat, and she couldn't bring herself to follow Jolie's nod. "Yeah. I do."

"But?"

"But Devin is hiring a new bodyguard for me today."

"Not if you tell him you want Gray," Rachel said.

"He lied about who he was."

Jolie laid her hand on Natalie's arm. "We've all been doing our share of lying, it seems. I'm sorry, Natalie. I was trying to keep you from getting hurt, and I did a lousy job of it. If I'd told you who Gray was from the beginning…"

Natalie held up a hand, cutting off her friend. "I'm sorry, too."

"Me, too," Rachel said. "And your brothers, well, they are who they are."

"They just wanted to protect me, too. I get it."

"So what are you going to do?" Jolie asked.

"You know, I'll bet he never *wanted* to lie to you."

"Probably not." Last night, Gray's lie had felt like a major betrayal. But if Natalie was honest with herself, she had to admit Gray's failure to tell her he was a hired bodyguard wasn't what bothered her most.

Natalie took a bite of cake and forced herself to swallow. She was sure it was delicious, but she couldn't appreciate the flavors. She doubted anything would taste good to her today. She wasn't used to being shot at. She wasn't used to being in danger. And she wasn't used to wanting a guy despite knowing he'd been hired to hang out with her... and there was a good chance he would turn around and leave as soon as the job was over.

"So?" Rachel prompted. "What happens between you two now?"

It was a good question. And one for which Natalie wasn't likely to get a reliable answer until she was out of danger, and Gray was free to walk away.

GRAY WAS SURPRISED when Natalie emerged from the bakery without Rachel and Jolie. He held up a hand, signaling for her to stop at the door and wait for him. After making another visual sweep of the area to confirm it was clear, he joined her at the door. "What's the problem? Where are Jolie and Rachel?"

"They're going to stay and try more cake."

"And you?"

She held her hand against her stomach. "I've had enough. Can we leave?"

"Of course." He strode beside her. When they reached his car, he opened the passenger door for her, then circled to the driver's side and climbed in. He started the car and pulled into traffic before he asked where they were going.

"I'm not sure. It depends, I guess." She stared out the window, her arms crossed over her chest, her fingers fidgeting with the sleeves of the sporty leather jacket she often wore on her days off.

"What does it depend on?"

She didn't speak, but her fidgeting moved to her feet.

"I can tell you've got something to say. Go ahead."

"I want to bring this to an end."

She'd said something to that effect last night, but it managed to make Gray's chest ache all over again. "When Devin gets another bodyguard in place—"

"That's not what I mean."

He raised his brows and waited for her to continue.

"I want this whole thing over, this threat to my family."

He nodded, still not sure where she was going with this. "I'm sure Ash and his fellow officers have a few new leads after last night."

"He does. And he's following up on those. But the St. Louis PD is like any other city police department these days, overworked and underfunded."

True enough. "So what do you have in mind?"

"I'm going to see what I can find out."

Now he hadn't seen *that* coming. "And how do you plan to do that?"

"I'm not sure yet. Talk to people? See if anyone noticed anything? I mean, this guy is after me. Maybe I'm the one in the best position to figure out who he is."

Gray wanted to tell her no, to shut her away and keep her safe from the world. "I might not have known you long, but I suspect you're going to do this whether I like it or not."

"Smart man."

"So if you're going to be skipping around

town talking to people, I'm going to be there with you."

She nodded. "You are my bodyguard."

"And you're okay with that suddenly?"

"You mean, do I realize I'm in danger now? Yes. Am I still angry with you for lying to me? A bit. But…"

"But?" he prompted.

"But I called Devin and told him I don't want another bodyguard. That I only want you. You saved my life twice, and I trust you. At least as far as that goes."

And he would make damn sure her trust was warranted. "So where do we start?"

She shot him a slightly embarrassed smile. "I don't have a clue. I was hoping you would."

He couldn't help but chuckle. This woman was something else. Even when she wasn't quite forgiving him, she still made him feel as if every moment around her was a gift.

He took a deep breath and reined in those sentiments. He'd let himself get distracted before, started thinking of Natalie as his plaything rather than someone he had been hired to lay down his life if necessary to protect. He wasn't going to make that mistake again. He needed to be ready to take care of her, not focus on his own needs. Her life depended on it. "This started with your paintings being slashed. What if we start there, too?"

"Go on."

"You mentioned an art dealer who wanted to show your work, and you turned him down."

"Maxim Miles. But I can't imagine why he even wanted them, let alone why he would try to kill me. They aren't exactly commercial."

"Judging from what I saw, they were pretty amazing."

She shook her head, as if to say he had no idea how to evaluate art.

He supposed he didn't. "I know I'm not an expert, but those paintings were beautiful. Haunting."

"But why would he destroy them?"

"Maybe he didn't destroy them all. You said yourself that you weren't sure if they were all there."

"I said that to the police, not you."

He gave a shrug, not crazy about reminding her of the secret he'd kept.

"And my brothers passed it along to you."

He nodded. "What if he took some of them and vandalized the rest to hide what he'd taken? You said he sold work for you before, right?"

"He even bought a few of my paintings for himself."

This was seeming like more of a lead all the time. "And what tends to happen to the work of artists who…" He stopped himself. His theory wasn't bad, but he couldn't quite bring himself to lay out the rest of the scenario.

"Artists who die? Especially in a dramatic fashion when their family has been all over the news for months?" Apparently Natalie wasn't quite so squeamish.

"If that is his plan—"

"To kill me?"

"Or to make it look like someone is trying to kill you. All he needs is the publicity in order to inflate the price."

Natalie nodded for him to go on.

"If that is his plan, he's only taken his first step last night."

She frowned. "Unless…"

"What?"

"I keep thinking about that woman in the powder-blue sweatshirt. I never saw her face, you know. She was kind of big, and the sweatshirt was very shapeless."

"You're thinking it might have been a man?"

"It might have been Max. I really can't say."

"But pushing you into traffic didn't do the trick, so he escalated to shooting. Could be. And he would have seen you with me, so he might have followed me and staked out my place. Then he was already familiar with it when I took you there last night."

Awkward silence dropped like a curtain between them. Gray felt horrible about how last night had turned out. It never should have happened. He never should have let things go that far. But he'd apologized several times already, and he sensed another round was the last thing Natalie wanted. "If that scenario is even close, Max couldn't have sold the paintings yet."

Natalie turned to him, eyes sparking. "They have to be in the gallery somewhere. They'd probably be in his office."

"Can we get in there somehow?"

She pursed her lips. "Maybe."

"What do you have in mind?"

She laid out a rough plan for him. It wouldn't be easy to pull off, but it just might work.

Gray nodded his approval. "Who knows, maybe we'll have this mess all sorted out, and before you know it, you won't need a bodyguard anymore."

She pressed her lips into a line and nodded, but instead of the excitement and grit he'd seen a second ago, she looked strangely sad.

MAXIM MILES OWNED an art studio in the fashionable Central West End in Saint Louis. Natalie had always loved the neighborhood. Even now, looking up at the glittering green dome of the Cathedral Basilica of Saint Louis gave her a feeling of awe and excitement. Too bad the prospect of seeing Max Miles again did not.

They made their way through the neighborhood. Turning down the tree-lined street where Max's gallery was located, Natalie wished she could reach out and grab Gray's hand. That physical reassurance that he was there with her would help her jittery nerves. At least she liked to imagine so. Deep down she suspected she was fooling herself.

"Is this it?" Gray's steps slowed.

Natalie focused on the row of shops and upscale restaurants. Delicious scents drifted from a bistro on the corner. Two doors down, the familiar white wood columns rose into the sky and curled into carved swirls like decorations on a wedding cake. "Yes, this is it."

He held the door open for her.

She took a deep breath and stepped inside.

The interior of the gallery was also just how she remembered it. Muted colors made the walls, flooring and ceiling fade into the background. Sophisticated lighting enhanced paintings, photography and sculpture displayed throughout the rooms. The scent of jasmine and soft lilt of classical music made the space feel expensive and sexy at once.

She'd been so excited when Max had first accepted one of her paintings, a stylized vision of the Kendall Estate's shade garden in black, white and deep greens. She'd been over the moon when he'd given her her first real show. Now she wished she'd never met the man.

"Don't tell me." Max stepped from behind a sculpture of a nude made from swirls of silver metal. He was still thin. His hairpiece was still too dark and too full. His black suit, shirt and tie had the same easy elegance. And his face still held the same hard smile. "Isn't this a coincidence? After all this time, you finally have something for me."

"No, I don't," Natalie said. She tried not to enjoy his fallen expression too much.

"Then you are here to buy?" He glanced at Gray, as if it was no question that the man would be wielding the checkbook, even though he knew full well Natalie could buy her own art.

Gray nodded, as they'd agreed. "I'm here to buy some of Natalie's paintings, in fact."

Max's eyebrows shot toward his synthetic hairline. "You have the artist here, and yet you want to buy from me?"

"She won't sell anything she has. But she said you used to show her work and might have some now."

The excuse sounded unbelievable, contrived and for a second, Natalie thought the art dealer would call Gray on it.

Instead, Max shrugged. "I did show her work. I would still be showing her work if she would cooperate."

Gray shook his head. "Artists are so fickle and eccentric."

"Exactly."

Natalie could feel her cheeks starting to heat. She was pretty sure this was an act, and Gray didn't really feel that way about her. But she supposed it didn't matter. When they found out who was trying to kill her and she no longer needed a bodyguard, then she would know the truth. Then Gray would either walk away or not. "So what is it, Max? Do you have any of my paintings or not?"

"I believe I might."

Natalie peered up at Gray. "I can tell you if he is charging too much."

Max held up a hand. The glow from a recessed light glinted off several gaudy rings. "Your job is to make the art, my dear. My job is to sell it. I will not haggle about price with you. Either I show him alone, or I do not show him anything."

Gray shot Natalie an apologetic glance, then he smiled at Max. "I don't need an advisor."

"Gray."

"We'll just be a few moments. Have a look around. See if there's something here you like." Gray looked back to Max. "Lead the way."

If Gray's placating tone had not been part of their plan, Natalie might just have to slap him. As it was, Max led him away to one of the back storage rooms. Before the door closed, she caught the sound of Max issuing orders to his assistant in the back, and then Natalie was alone.

When she'd dealt with Max, he'd had only one assistant working during the week and used part-time help for special events. She hoped that was still the case.

She pulled in a calming breath and took off in the direction of Max's personal office. Rounding an abstract sculpture made from hammered copper, heavy wire and stone, she slowed her steps. Once she turned down the hall that led to the office, she could no longer say she was checking out the pieces of art. Max would know she was snooping. She stopped at the mouth of the hall, listening for any movement.

Not hearing any sign of life, she stepped quickly down the hall and found Max's office door. The door was locked, as usual, with a keypad doorknob. She punched in the old code she remembered him using, a string of nines, and tried the door.

It held fast.

So Max had changed the digits in his code. That shouldn't surprise her. She punched in his birthdate.

Nothing. She tried his birthdate along with the date he'd opened the gallery.

No good. She was nearly out of options when she had an idea. She pulled out her iPhone. Checking to see which numbers corresponded to which letters on a standard telephone, she typed in *Miles*. It didn't budge. She typed in *money*.

The lever turned under her hand.

Figured. She slipped into the dim office and closed the door behind her.

Nearly as large as one of the small gallery showrooms, Max's office held a large desk, a leather couch, a wide credenza and jumbles of boxes and stacks of paintings.

How would she find anything in this mess? She had no idea. But she didn't have time to sit around and reason it out.

She started with the closest pile of paintings. Each was stored in protective crates or other types of packing. She didn't have enough time to sort through all of these. By the time she was able to reveal even one painting, Gray and Max would be finished with their business and looking for her. There had to be a faster way.

She focused on breathing. In, two, three, four. Out, two, three, four. Her pulse throbbed in her ears, making it hard to hear any noises outside the room.

If Max had taken anything from her house, he wouldn't have had the paintings long. He also wouldn't want them to get tangled up with the other consignments. He'd hide them someplace special.

She threaded through the stacks of artwork and slipped behind his desk. Two cartons leaned up against the credenza, plenty big enough for each to hold one of her paintings.

Voices erupted outside the door.

Natalie tried to think, to breathe. Her pulse pounded in her ears. She couldn't hear if one of the voices belonged to Max or someone else, but it didn't really matter. There was no talking her way out of this one. Losing her way while looking for the restroom wasn't going to cover breaking into a locked and darkened office.

The door rattled as if someone was punching in the code.

She dropped to her hands and knees and shuffled closer to the desk. She forced her breathing to slow. She wasn't alone. She had to remember that. Gray was here, and he was armed. He wouldn't let Max hurt her.

The pressure in the room changed, and Natalie could tell whoever was at the door had opened it and was inside the room.

"I'll be with you in just a moment."

Max.

Footsteps shuffled toward her followed by the scrape of crates rubbing against one another.

"My time is valuable." Gray's voice

boomed from the doorway. "You said this phone call would only take a minute."

Natalie let out the breath she hadn't been aware she was holding. Gray would get Max out of the office. He would give her time to look at the contents of the cartons. She just had to make sure Max didn't discover her before Gray could coax him back into the storeroom.

"You're a valuable customer, Mr. Scott. Let me find what I'm looking for. I think you'll be pleased."

"I'd better be, because this seems to be taking forever."

"Trust me, you will be. And since Natalie is here, she can verify them for you."

Verify them? He must be talking about her paintings. Natalie glanced at the cartons behind the desk. In the dim light filtering through the blinds, she could barely make out a scrawled name in the corner. She leaned closer, squinting.

"Ahh, yes. I remember where I tucked them."

She spied the name and her breath caught in her throat. *Demetrius Jones.* It had been a long time since she'd thought of him, but not long enough.

Footsteps rounded the desk, coming toward her.

She squeezed past the chair and slipped into the darkness under the desk. Keeping her breathing shallow, she willed Max not to hear the mad thump of her heart.

Max's Bruno Magli shoes gleamed even in the dim light. He stepped straight to the cartons Natalie had found, the ones Demetrius had sent him. He picked them up, straightened and paused.

She tried to shrink farther back under the desk. She couldn't tell how long he stood there, but it seemed like forever. Finally he stepped around the desk, left the office and closed the door behind him and Gray.

Natalie sagged against the desk. She'd thought for sure he'd see her, sense that she was there. But now that he hadn't, she had another problem. Not only had he taken the paintings, based on what he'd said to Gray, he was taking them out to the main gallery to show her.

And she wasn't there.

She rolled the chair back and scrambled out from under the desk. Bits of paper packing clung to her skirt, tights and boots. One look and Max would wonder why she'd been crawling on the floor. She brushed her clothing and legs. Fairly certain she was clean, she wound through the maze of crates scattering the floor. She reached the door and paused, hand on knob, to listen.

No sound came from the hall. Either Gray had convinced Max to go back to the storeroom, or they were now about to realize she was no longer in the main gallery.

She had to make up a cover story. And she had to hurry.

She pushed down on the lever and pulled open the door. Taking a deep breath, she stepped out into the hall.

"So there you are. What a surprise." Max's voice was as hard as his eyes.

Chapter Ten

"What were you doing in my office?"

Natalie's heartbeat stuttered in her chest. She tried for words, but she couldn't grasp any that made sense. Her fallback, the bathroom excuse, obviously wouldn't fly. She looked past Max and focused on Gray at the end of the hall.

He gave her a tight smile, as if everything was under perfect control.

"No explanation? Then I can only assume you and your friend here are trying to rob me." Max reached for his phone. "I'm calling the police."

"Go ahead." Gray stepped toward Max. At well over six feet, Gray towered over him. "And when you do, ask for Natalie's brother, Detective Ash Kendall. I'm sure he'd like to know why you vandalized her studio, destroyed half a dozen paintings and stole a couple more."

Max's eyebrows shot toward his synthetic hairline. "What are you talking about?"

Natalie looked at Gray as well, waiting for the explanation.

"You broke into Natalie's house and vandalized some of her paintings and stole others. Don't bother denying it."

"Okay, I won't bother. But then I have nothing to say, because I wasn't there."

Gray picked up one of the cartons Max had taken from the office. He reached inside and pulled out a canvas.

Natalie could have sworn Max turned a shade paler. After all the times Max Miles had tried to bully her, she couldn't help feeling as if she was finally getting a little justice.

Gray turned the canvas around.

It was a painting of a dark figure in a shadowy room. A drapery floated in the background, white and tattered, and red pooled on the floor.

"Where did you get this?" Natalie demanded.

"Demetrius Jones brought it in yesterday. He said it was one of yours."

Natalie's face felt hot. She could feel Gray watching her, waiting for some kind of explanation. "Is there another in the other crate?"

Max nodded.

Gray pulled out his phone. "Don't bother making that call to the police, Miles. I'll make it for you."

"Wait." Natalie held up a hand.

Gray paused, questions in his eyes.

Natalie looked once again at the painting. The dark colors. The shadowy figure just like the one she'd painted so many times. The bright red of blood. "This painting isn't one of mine."

NATALIE'S STATEMENT didn't make sense. Gray shook his head and took another look at the painting. Then he returned his gaze to Natalie's face. "What do you mean, it isn't yours?"

"Just that. I didn't paint this."

Maxim Miles bit out a curse. "I should have known it. I never should have believed that crook."

"What crook would that be?" Gray asked.

"Demetrius Jones. He brought these in yesterday. Said he got them from Natalie. That he finally talked her into selling some of her newer work. I suspected he was trying to pull something over on me, as usual. Should have told him to get the hell out. Should have known from the beginning it wasn't on the up-and-up."

Gray got the idea Max was a regular expert when it came to things that weren't on the up-and-up. He turned away from Max and focused on Natalie. "You didn't paint this?"

She shook her head. "Demetri, he's an artist, too."

Max let out a bark of a laugh. "He's not *really* an artist, babe. Let's be honest. He's a wannabe who thought that by dating you he could steal a little of your talent. Or at least your connections. And I haven't been able to get rid of him since."

So he'd tried to become successful by using Natalie. Was that what these paintings were about, too? "Am I really the only one who has seen your newer paintings?" Gray asked.

"Except for Ash and the officers who were with him the night of the break-in, yes. You're the only one."

"Then if this is a copy that Demetri painted in order to pass it off as one of yours, when did he see the paintings?"

Natalie nodded. "The night he broke into my cottage and vandalized my studio."

As soon as they left The Miles Gallery, Gray turned to Natalie. "Do you know where Demetri lives?"

She nodded. "I got a look at the mailing

label on one of those cartons. It's not too far away. You want to go have a talk?" She seemed less than enthusiastic about the idea.

"I think it might be enlightening," he admitted. "But if you'd rather not, we could just let Ash know and be done with it."

"No. I want to see his face when he tries to explain his way out of this one."

Gray could tell there was a significant history between Demetri and Natalie. And somewhere deep inside, he couldn't prevent a twinge of jealousy. He wanted to find the truth, but he had to admit he also wanted to size up this guy. Find out what Natalie saw in him.

"You want to tell me about him?"

"There's not much to tell." Natalie's cheeks shone pink. Combined with the way she was avoiding looking him in the eye, Gray doubted the bloom of color was solely due to the wind.

"Is what Miles said true?"

"What, that he was my boyfriend? That he took advantage of me?" She let out a long, shaky sigh. "Yeah, it's true. Demetri was never that interested in me. He wanted my connections. He wanted my family's money. He wanted me to teach him what I knew. And when I did, he left. It wasn't one of the best times in my life."

"I'm sorry."

She shrugged, as if her history with this guy meant nothing.

Gray didn't buy it. He'd seen the humiliation in her face and the hurt in her voice. The thought of some idiot hurting her made him want to turn his fists on that idiot. If anyone deserved a good man who would put her before his own selfish wants, it was Natalie. Why she had to be tangled up with a loser like this guy obviously was, he'd never know. "He shouldn't have used you like that."

"It could have been worse."

"How?"

"I could have actually been in love with him."

He felt those words like a kick to the gut. Hadn't Devin warned him about just such circumstances? At least when she'd found out he was her bodyguard, she hadn't been in love with him. At least he hadn't hurt her that much. "Do you think Demetri might resort to murder?"

"I doubt it."

"You don't sound sure."

"I'm not sure of anything anymore."

"Are you sure you feel up to talking to him?"

"I might not have had him figured out all those years ago, but he can't fool me now."

They walked in silence until Natalie stopped in front of a shop selling beeswax candles and other useless gifts. She gestured to a narrow staircase leading to the floor above the shop.

Demetri Jones lived in one of the tiniest apartments Gray had ever seen, unexpected since the tree-lined streets of the prestigious neighborhood itself were populated with stately homes and upscale shops and restaurants. Even more surprising was the fact that Demetri was not a small man. With the face and charm of a movie star and the muscle of a bodybuilder, he was almost as tall as Gray and his shoulders were nearly as wide.

At least they could be pretty sure he wasn't the person wearing the light blue sweatshirt who'd pushed Natalie into traffic.

He frowned at Gray, but when he spotted Natalie, he opened the door as wide as his smile. "Babe."

Gray hated him even more.

Natalie entered the apartment and stepped away from the big man's attempt at a hug. "We have something to talk to you about."

"Who's *we?*"

Gray pushed his way in behind Natalie. "We hear you've been copying Natalie's paintings and trying to sell them as hers."

Demetri didn't even blink. In fact, his smile got a little wider. "I'm just trying to make a living. You can't blame me."

Natalie plopped her hands on her hips. "Where did see my paintings, Demetri?"

"What do you mean, where'd I see your paintings. At your place, baby."

"I never showed them to you. Not my new work. I never showed that to anyone."

"You saw them at Natalie's house almost a week ago, didn't you?" Demetri might be almost as big as Gray, but that didn't mean much. Gray had taken men his size. Even with his bad knee and other injuries from the incident in Yemen, he still had the strength.

His eyebrows pulled low and he looked at Gray as if he'd just spouted gibberish. "A week?"

Gray took a step forward. "You shredded most of them. And took a couple, too. Where are they, Demetri?"

"What are you talking about?"

"And there's more, too. You hired or at least convinced someone to push Natalie into the street. You've been lurking around outside her cottage at night. And last night you shot up my apartment."

Demetri shook his head. He shot Natalie a desperate look. "Who is this guy?"

Natalie ignored the question. "Explain, Demetri."

He threw out his hands, palms up. "Why would I do any of that?"

"You're copying her paintings. You want to increase their value."

He actually had the nerve to smile. "You got that part right. What can I say? The Christmas Eve Murders have been in the news. But the rest of what you were saying... I don't know anything about that stuff."

"Then when did you see my paintings? The newer ones? Like the ones you forged and tried to sell to Max."

"Oh, damn. You talked to Max? You didn't tell him those paintings I sent him aren't yours, did you?"

"Of course, I did. They aren't mine. They aren't even all that close to mine."

"Oh, great. Thanks a lot, Natalie. I needed that money. Now what am I supposed to do?"

Gray had enough. Of this guy's lies, of him calling Natalie *babe* and most of all of the insensitive comments he let fall from his mouth.

Gray lunged forward. Bringing the flat of his forearm up under Demetri's chin, he pushed the big man back and pinned him against the hallway's wall. "Unless you want to start a little trouble, you need to answer. Where and when did you see those paintings?"

"Hey, slow down, man," he said in a strangled voice.

"When and where?" Gray repeated.

"Let up. Let up. I'll answer your damn questions."

Gray lowered his arm and took a step back.

Demetri's movie-star handsome face was flushed. He rubbed his throat with a hand. "I didn't see them a week ago. But I did get a glimpse back when Natalie and me were an item."

Beside him, Natalie shuffled her feet on the floor. She brushed her hair back from her eyes. "I never showed you my paintings."

"I didn't say you showed me."

Gray narrowed his eyes on the man. "How did you see them?"

Demetri gave him a half smile. "She ever tell you about her nightmares?"

Gray glanced at Natalie.

"So you haven't slept with her then, have you?" He shot Gray a taunting smile.

Gray had the urge to wipe it right off his face.

She looked to the floor and once again swiped her hand across her cheek. "Answer the question, Demetri."

"Oh, shouldn't I kiss and tell?"

The only thing keeping Gray from punching the guy in the mouth was that he needed it to talk. "Answer the question."

"I snuck a peek. I was curious."

"In her house a few days ago, we know."

"No, after we'd had some great sex." Another grin. "I had to get a look. You can't blame me. I was in her bed plenty of times when she had those nightmares. And afterward, she didn't sleep. She just went into her studio and locked the door. When she came out in the morning, she always had paint on her fingers and clothes. Shades of black and gray and blood...bloodred. I was curious. So one day I peeked. Disturbing stuff."

Natalie avoided meeting Gray's eyes.

"So I need some cash, and I thought I might be able to find a gallery interested in stuff like that," Demetri drawled on. "But if

I didn't, I figured I could always try some kind of house of horror. That's where that kind of art really belongs."

Chapter Eleven

Gray didn't say anything for three blocks, and neither did Natalie. They walked through the streets, back in the direction of his car. The sun now hid behind hazy clouds, and the wind had turned cool. The scent of Italian herbs drifted from a gourmet pizza place, and Gray's stomach growled, despite the fact that he didn't feel hungry. He stole a glance at Natalie.

She stared straight ahead, her hair swirling around her cheeks. Tears glistened in her eyes and streaked paths down her cheeks.

Somehow he doubted it was all due to the wind. "Do you want to tell me about these nightmares?"

"Not really, no."

He knew she wanted him to back off. A gentleman probably would. But since that wasn't something he'd ever been accused of being, he pushed on. "Do they have something to do with your parents' murders?"

She shook her head, but Gray got the idea the gesture didn't necessarily mean her answer was no.

"Don't want to talk about it?"

"I'm sorry. I just can't."

"That's fair."

They returned to silence, completing another block. The cloudy sky turned to rain, small drops pattering on their heads and darkening sidewalks and streets. The Cathedral Basilica of Saint Louis's dome towered in front of them, glistening almost as brightly in the rain as it had in the sun. The car wasn't far now, but Gray wasn't ready to bring Natalie home. He had a hunch she would hide out in her bedroom or studio and he would never find out about the paintings and nightmares. And maybe as a simple bodyguard he didn't need to know what was so troubling and painful to his client. But as a man, he wanted to help. "Let's step in out of the rain."

She opened her mouth to protest.

He kept talking. "I haven't seen the mosaics for a long time. It'll just take a minute. This shower looks like it will blow over pretty quickly."

She nodded, and they ducked inside.

The interior of the cathedral was as amazing as he remembered. Every inch of the place seemed to be covered with mosaics made from tiny tiles. It smelled like serenity and candle wax. Quiet seemed to echo from every corner, and except for a few people taking in the famous site, just as they were, the place felt quiet, safe, calm.

He led Natalie to a secluded hallway off the cathedral's nave. "I want you to know you can talk to me, Natalie. It seems like there are a lot of things you're keeping bottled up inside. It might help to let some of that out."

She didn't say anything, just kept moving through the hall, very slowly, taking in the artwork. Gray had nearly given up when she finally spoke. "I don't know, sometimes…"

"Sometimes what?" he prompted.

"Sometimes I wonder if the Kendalls aren't all just marked or something."

"Because of your parents?"

"And everything else that's happened since DNA tests showed Rick Campbell didn't kill them. I mean, we still don't know who really murdered them. He's still out there."

That had to be hard. So hard, Gray didn't know how any of the Kendalls dealt with it as well as they had. There was also another thought that had been bothering him. It started as an uneasy feeling, but it had grown as they'd talked to Max and then Demetri. "Do you think it might be the person who shot at you?"

She gave a hint of a shrug. "And pushed me into traffic? I don't know. I don't think it was Max or Demetri, though."

"Me, either. If Max had any of your real paintings, he would have shown them to me. Also, I can't see that guy ever destroying artwork. Not when he could sell it."

"I agree." She shrugged and wrapped her arms around herself, as if she was chilled from the rain.

He took off his jacket and draped it over her.

"Now you're going to be cold."

"I'll manage."

She stopped and looked up into his eyes. "It could be the same person, couldn't it? Someone who wants to silence our family so he will never be discovered."

Gray frowned. It was a theory, but he wasn't sure it added up. "I thought the people who were after your brothers were stopped."

"They were." She thought for a moment. "So I suppose that can't be the reason they were targeted."

An uneasy feeling tensed his shoulders and

neck. "But you're thinking that might be the reason someone is trying to kill you?"

"It sounds silly, doesn't it?"

"It doesn't sound silly at all. It sounds like there's a lot you haven't told me."

Ignoring his prompt, she sighed and scuffed her shoes on the marble floor. "Sometimes I wonder if things will ever be normal again."

"So you don't have to have a bodyguard anymore?"

She looked away from him, but once again he caught a sense of sadness in her expression.

Strange. Knowing how upset she'd been at learning she had a bodyguard, he'd think the idea of him gone would cheer her. After all, last night at his apartment and this morning at the bakery, she'd made it perfectly clear that while she might need him in the short term, as soon as she didn't have someone shoving her into moving cars, taking potshots and running around outside her cottage at night, she would be all too happy to tell him goodbye. "Are you having a change of heart?"

"Over what?"

"You look so sad at the idea of not needing a bodyguard."

"It's not that."

He tried not to show his disappointment. "What is it then?"

"I wish none of this was happening. I wish you weren't my bodyguard. I wish you could be what I thought you were. Just a guy I like."

He nodded. "I wish that, too."

"But it's not possible, is it?"

He thought about how wrapped up in her he'd been when she was pushed into traffic, so wrapped up he hadn't gotten as much of a look at the person following as she had. He'd ignored that warning sign. Ignored it until the shots came crashing through his bedroom window, shots that had almost killed her. "To keep you safe, I have to make sacrifices."

"Sacrifices?"

"I have to pay more attention to everything around us. I'm afraid when I'm kissing you, that's all I can think about."

She gave him a sad smile. "I like that."

"Then why do I get the feeling that you don't believe me?"

"It's not you. I just don't have the best of track records when it comes to men. At least the ones I like."

After this afternoon, he could see why. "Maybe you shouldn't like them in the first place."

"You're talking about Demetri. Yeah,

he's a jerk. I'm not sure what I was thinking dating him. No, not true. I wanted to believe he liked me. He didn't fool me as much as I fooled myself."

"I'm sure a lot of men like you, Natalie." Him included. No, him especially.

"Thanks. But that's not it, really. The problem is finding a man who will stick around. It seems like whenever I start to really like a guy, he pulls away."

"I'm not pulling away. I mean, not on purpose, not by choice."

"I know. But I end up alone either way." She gave a shrug, as if it was no big deal.

He didn't buy it. Not for a second. "For what it's worth, if I really was that regular guy who worked with alarm systems, I wouldn't pull away."

"So it's the job."

"Yes." But even as he said the word, he knew it wasn't true. It wasn't simply a matter of being her bodyguard. It was about who he was. What he had to prove. "And no."

She crooked a brow. "You said you blamed yourself for your buddy's death."

He nodded. She'd connected the dots almost as if she could read his mind. But he didn't want to talk about Jimbo. Just the memory of what had happened off the coast of Yemen still ached like an open wound. But he couldn't cut Natalie off. If he wanted her to open up to him, he had to be willing to open up to her. "At Jimbo's memorial service, his wife, Sherry, said something that really struck home."

"What?"

He swallowed, trying to rid himself of the thick feeling in his throat. It didn't do any good. Sherry had lashed out at him due to anger and grief, but that didn't make her words untrue. "She said I should have died instead of her husband. She said I only survived because I wasn't willing to make the kind of sacrifice Jimbo made."

"What a horrible thing to say."

"It's true." It hurt to say those words out loud, especially to Natalie, but there they were.

She shook her head. "It's not."

"You don't know me, Natalie. I grew up with everything. Money. Enough smarts to do well in school. Opportunities to do anything I wanted. I've never had to sacrifice for anything, not my entire life."

"So you grew up wealthy. So did I."

Now it was his turn for a head shake. "You're very different from me."

"How?"

"First, your father was a self-made man. He sacrificed a lot to build Kendall Communications."

"So did my uncle and my brother. But I didn't."

"I'm willing to bet you sacrificed time with your dad. I'll bet he was never home."

"No, I suppose he wasn't. My memory of my parents is a little foggy. I was only six when they died." She bit her bottom lip and blinked as if driving back tears. "But I sometimes wonder if they were very happy. I have shadowy memories, but I don't know if they're all that accurate. I asked my aunt, but she kind of avoided the whole topic."

"That's the other thing. You lost both your parents so young. I can't imagine a bigger sacrifice."

She turned her face to the side, but she couldn't hide her tears.

He felt for Natalie. He couldn't imagine losing his parents at age six. He couldn't imagine losing his parents at all. Right now they were in Italy, exploring Venice. But they would be back to celebrate Christmas. He could count on it. And that was an assurance Natalie would never have. "So you see, we're very different."

"But you jumped into heavy traffic to save

me. And you risked your life to get me out of the line of fire last night."

"It's my job."

She narrowed her eyes on him, as if she could see right through his defenses and into his heart. "Is that why you took the job? To prove you can sacrifice your life like your friend did?"

He'd asked himself that countless times. And each time, he came up with the same answer. "Probably."

"You know, even if you do manage to get yourself killed, it won't bring your friend back."

His chest felt hollow. "I know that. It also won't erase my failure in Yemen."

"But you didn't fail. You said you kept the ship from being bombed."

"I lost men."

"It isn't just about sacrifice then. You blame yourself for your friend's death."

He didn't know what to say. Of course he did. And he knew nothing he could ever do would change the fact that Jimbo was dead, when it should have been him.

"That's what my nightmares are about."

Her voice was quiet, almost a whisper, and at first he wasn't sure what she said. "The nightmares you painted?"

She nodded. "I could have stopped my parents' murders."

He studied her for a moment, not sure what to make of her statement. He'd heard of children blaming themselves for their parents' divorce. He supposed a child could feel as if she should have stopped a murder, too. But Natalie was no longer a child. Surely she could see that a little girl could never wield such power. "You were six years old."

"Someone came into my room that night. At first, I thought it was Santa. It was Christmas Eve, you know. Then when I saw he wasn't fat and didn't have a big beard, I figured it was my dad. When he worked late, he'd sometimes come in and check on me before he went to bed."

"But it wasn't your dad?"

"I don't think so. I think it was their murderer."

The man's face cloaked in shadow. The dark figure in her paintings. "How do you know it was the killer?"

"I don't, really. It's just a feeling." She stared at the tiles covering the walls and arching across the ceiling.

Gray had to wonder if she was looking at the mosaics at all, or if she only saw her memories. "You can't blame yourself for a hunch you're having twenty years after the fact."

Natalie glanced at him for a second and then looked away.

She wasn't going to let herself off the hook. At least not because of what he had to say. "What do you remember? What did the man do?"

"He was sitting on the edge of my bed when I woke up. He was watching me." She bit her bottom lip.

"Do you remember what he looked like? Any facial features? What he was wearing?"

She shook her head. "There was a light in the hall behind him. It was dim, but compared to the darkness in my room everything seemed black. I could only see his silhouette, just enough to know he wasn't Santa."

"So he sat on your bed. What else do you remember?"

She looked past Gray, as if back in her bedroom all those years ago. "I remember him touching my hair, very gently, as if I was the most precious thing in the world to him. And he smiled at me. I couldn't see his face, not really, but I could feel his smile. It felt like a nice smile."

"Did your dad usually do that kind of thing when he checked on you?"

She gave her head a little shake. "He never did. He would just peek in the doorway for a few seconds, then leave. But I always wanted him to sit on my bed, to check on me. I think that's why I believed it was my father. I *wanted* it to be him."

So far, he couldn't see a reason she was so certain it wasn't her father. The fact that he usually checked on her from a distance didn't mean he hadn't sat on her bed that night. There had to be more. "Did he say anything?"

"*Go back to sleep*. That's what he said."

"Did you recognize his voice?"

"That's just it. His voice wasn't my dad's." She focused on Gray, her eyes shining with unshed tears. "I should have screamed. Right then, I should have screamed as loud as I could. If I had, my parents would still be here."

Gray's throat ached. He wanted to say something, but he didn't know what. He wanted to wrap her in his arms and make everything better, but he knew that wasn't so simple. Instead, he said nothing, did nothing, just waited for her to continue if she chose.

She looked away from him, took a deep breath and swiped at her eyes with her fingertips.

The air in the basilica was still as that of a tomb, and for a long time there was no sound besides her ragged breathing. He could smell the fragrance of her hair, something slightly floral, sweet. He wondered if her skin smelled the same way. He wondered what she would do if he leaned in close and nuzzled her neck, if he took her in his arms. He wondered if he could help ease her pain, if anyone could.

Finally she turned back to look at him, shadows cupping her reddened eyes.

"It's okay," he said, his voice the slightest whisper.

She shook her head. "No. It will never be okay. I should have screamed, but I didn't make a sound. I just pretended it was my daddy who touched my hair, who looked at me like that. And early the next morning, I went into my parents' bedroom to see if they were ready to go down to the tree and see what Santa brought, and I found them. Dead."

Chapter Twelve

The days running up to Ash and Rachel's wedding were uneventful, much to Natalie's relief. Gray moved into her cottage and slept on the sofa, and it was all she could do to keep herself from wandering out in the middle of the night to see what might happen.

Nearly every night she dreamed of lying naked on his bed, the moonlight illuminating his face as he watched her. Sometimes she touched herself in her dream, massaging her breasts and sliding her fingers between her legs. Sometimes she just lay there with splayed thighs and begged him to join her. But he never did. And every time, after she'd pleasured herself in front of him or grown exhausted from begging, every single time, he turned away from her, walked out and left her alone in the room.

She didn't need a psychology degree to figure out the meaning of that one.

She leaned close to the bathroom mirror and finished putting on her second coat of waterproof mascara. That day in the basilica, the way she'd poured out her heart to Gray, had changed things between them. But she suspected it was really her it had changed. She wanted Gray more each day. And while he did seem in tune with her and as wonderful as ever, there was a distance, too. A physical one, for sure. But also an emotional uncertainty. As if neither one of them knew what happened next and neither one was bold enough to take that step, even if they did.

She wasn't going to dwell on her impossible longings today. Nor her insecurities. Nor the threat to her life, the only reason Gray was still with her. Today was her brother's wedding, and she couldn't wait to get to the chapel they'd chosen for the ceremony and into that beautiful dress.

It was a day to celebrate love.

She found Gray waiting in the living room. Dressed in one of the most gorgeous tuxedos she'd ever seen, he looked like a movie star waiting to take a red-carpet stroll.

"You're wearing that?" she joked.

He turned a smile on her. It faded to confusion as he took in her jeans, blouse and cardigan. "Ready to go?" He glanced at his watch.

"Yup. How do I look?" She did a pirouette. She started laughing before she'd completed a three-sixty. "We're changing into our dresses at the chapel. That way they don't get wrinkled before the ceremony."

"I knew that." He gave a chuckle and stretched his arm out as if dramatically ushering her out the door. His tuxedo jacket opened with the gesture, revealing a crisp white shirt and a black holstered gun.

Natalie swallowed, her throat dry. She'd gotten used to Gray being armed, even gotten used to having a bodyguard. But somehow it was still a little sobering to see his weapon even under his festive, formal attire.

A reminder of reality.

The ride to the chapel didn't take long. As they parked outside and walked to the front steps, Natalie couldn't help thinking how lucky Ash and Rachel were to find such a lovely place in such a short time. The best wedding venues in St. Louis tended to book up a year in advance and often more. And this chapel, with its classic spire and picture-perfect front steps, was one of the most charming Natalie had ever seen.

A huge graveyard flanked the building

and stretched several lots deep. But due to the many trees and amazing landscaping, it looked more like an expansive garden than a cemetery. It really was perfect. As bad as she felt for whoever the couple was who had to cancel their wedding, she was glad Ash and Rachel had the opportunity to slip into their place.

They climbed the steps and entered the front doors. Natalie led Gray through the narthex and into the nave. The first thing Natalie noticed was the beautiful yet simple stonework behind the altar. The second thing was the scent.

The flowers in the graveyard gardens outside were winding down for the winter, but the altar was blooming with breathtaking arrangements of roses and seasonal planters of chrysanthemums. Two tables behind the back pews held low boxes filled with boutonnieres and corsages ready for the family and wedding party to don when they arrived.

People were scattered throughout the chapel. A string quartet warmed up just to the right of the altar, playing scales and tuning their instruments. Aunt Angela bustled down the center aisle, adjusting pew bows. Uncle Craig stood grimacing while the florist pinned a white rose to the lapel of his tux. A few of Ash's friends from the force stood joking in the corner and stashing bags of streamers, clattering cans and who-knew-what that Natalie assumed would soon festoon Ash's car.

"So where do you need to be?" Gray said, voice clipped and businesslike.

"The church office. Rachel and Jolie are probably already there."

"All right." He turned to lead the way.

Natalie grabbed his arm. "Wait."

He turned back to look at her.

Nearly as soon as his gaze touched hers, it darted off, circling the room, checking the perimeter. Under his tux jacket, his muscles felt hard as rock.

"You're so tense."

"This place might not be huge, but there are a lot of ingresses, egresses. I have a lot to check before the wedding starts."

"Okay. Of course, I don't want to keep you. But there's one more thing." She plucked a boutonniere from one of the boxes.

"Oh, I don't need a flower."

She pulled the pins from the tape-wrapped stems. "Actually, you do. You may be my bodyguard, but today you're also my date."

His eyes met hers, and he gave her a little smile. "Then by all means."

She didn't remember a time when she was so clumsy. After sticking her fingertips twice and Gray's chest once, she finally secured the rose.

"How does it look?"

She stepped back and took him in. The tux skimmed over his broad shoulders and muscular body like it had been tailored specifically for him, which it probably had. Add that to being a good-looking man anyway, and the complete picture put any image of red-carpet movie stars she'd ever seen to shame. She couldn't resist giving him a flirty smile. "It'll do."

He chuckled. "Probably the most I can hope for."

She tried to keep a tight rein on her own hopes. And her own tongue. "I'd better go. Where are you going to be?"

"For the ceremony? Up there." He nodded to the back of the church.

She traced his gaze up to the balcony overlooking the pews.

"Your brother also arranged for additional security at the entrances. You'll be safe."

She brought her focus back to him. She couldn't help it. Just like with her thoughts, her eyes kept returning, as if pulled by a magnet. "I never doubted it. Not with you here."

Gray looked away first. "Go ahead. I can't wait to see you walk down the aisle."

A shiver peppered her skin. The man, tux, the flowers, the music—it was all straight from her fantasies. Whatever disappointment she felt at him breaking eye contact first was wiped away by the thought of him there, watching her as she walked down the aisle.

Of course, in her fantasies, he wouldn't be standing on the back balcony. He'd be at the altar.

GRAY HAD TO ADMIT, he wasn't looking forward to the wedding, not that he'd ever confess that to Natalie or any of the other Kendalls. Not even under pain of torture.

He was happy for Ash and Rachel. But a crowded church and a set time were like neon-sign invitations to anyone who wanted to cause trouble. The only thing that made his job at all easier was the fact that a large percentage of the guests happened to be cops, and most of them happened to be armed.

He checked in with Ash and the additional security. Standing at the entrance, he greeted guests as they arrived, as if he was head usher. Three of Ash's fellow cops took it from there, seating the guests in the chapel while the string quartet played Mozart. As the time for the wedding approached, Gray left the door to the outside security and the ushers and took his place in the balcony.

One of the ushers seated Natalie's aunt and uncle, then the bride's mother, and then the minister, Ash, Devin and a couple of men Gray didn't know filed in and stood at the altar. Natalie had a third brother, but although a woman at the cable news network had promised by phone to give Thad the message he was needed at home, he had yet to show. Gray couldn't help thinking that was a bit odd, even for a world-traveling reporter like Thad, but the Kendall family had taken it in stride.

The music soared and the women started filing down the aisle.

Gray didn't recognize two of them. Of course, he knew Devin's redheaded fiancée. And then there was Natalie, her straight, blond hair shining against the deep blue of her dress.

He had to admit, her power over him was disturbing. The moment she walked in the room, his attention riveted to her, her smile, the way she moved, every detail. He wanted her to turn around and look for him. He wanted to always be the man she looked for.

He gripped the rail in front of him, steadying himself. He couldn't let himself get carried away like this. His obligation was to keep Natalie safe, not take her for his own.

He tore his eyes from her and swept the crowd. He had to focus on the people below, their behavior. Any detail could cue him to a threat. The rest he couldn't think about. He forced all of it into the background, the sound of the minister's voice, the music, the vows. But despite his best efforts, he still found his eyes lingering on Natalie.

When the minister finally pronounced Ash and Rachel as husband and wife, Gray felt exhausted. He watched the wedding party file out and then descended the steps.

He moved through the receiving line with all the other guests, shaking hands and smiling. When he reached Natalie, she took him into a polite hug and it was all he could do to keep from pulling her closer. Instead, he whispered, "good job," into the silk of her hair and moved on to shake Devin's hand. After wishing the newlyweds well, he took up position at the base of the church steps and scanned the assemblage.

Two security guards flanked the gathering

crowd, the third still inside the church. The sun had started to dip behind the cityscape, and shadows stretched across the tombstones surrounding the church.

Gray eyed the happy couple, willing them to hurry it up. He hadn't liked the idea of a receiving line outdoors. But since the chapel was too small to accommodate one inside, he'd been overruled, and Ash had arranged for additional security instead. Now Gray just wanted this part of the tradition over and the Kendalls all safe in their cars, speeding toward the reception they'd planned for the evening. Maybe then he would let himself relax.

"Rose petals?" A little girl beamed up at Gray and pushed a small bag tied by a ribbon into his hand.

"Rose petals?" Gray echoed.

"To throw at the bride and groom. You know, instead of rice. Rice is bad for the birds."

"Thanks." He gave her a smile, and she scampered away to hand out more rose petals.

The receiving line broke up, and Natalie joined him at the bottom of the steps.

His smile grew. "Congratulations."

"For what?"

"For being the most beautiful bridesmaid."

"Gee thanks, but I'll bet Devin wouldn't agree."

Gray glanced at Natalie's older brother who stood arm in arm with Jolie. He could see the huge diamond on her finger from here. "She's beautiful, too. But I prefer blondes."

She smiled. "Thanks. But at a wedding, all eyes are on the bride." She looked back to her brother's new wife.

Ash and Rachel stood in the doorway of the church, poised to start down the steps to their car under a shower of rose petals.

"She's so lucky. Ash will always be there for her, and now they have a baby on the way." She drew in a shaky breath. Tears sparkled in her eyes, making them shine like emeralds. "And soon Jolie will be married to Devin, too."

"You're a romantic."

"I suppose so. I've always wanted someone just for me, you know? Someone to share things with. Someone to care for."

"Someone who will be there for you."

"Yes. Someone who will never leave."

He didn't want to tell her that love didn't mean people would never leave. He was no authority, anyway. Maybe some people did have that kind of bond. He didn't even know if he was capable. Or that someone like Natalie would even want to take a chance on him.

But he had to admit, spending all this time with Natalie, he was starting to understand the appeal. He almost had enough courage worked up to voice the thought when the first shot rang out.

Chapter Thirteen

Natalie heard the pop of gunfire, but for a second, she couldn't get her body to react.

Screams erupted around her. Many of the guests ran, colliding into one another, some falling. Rachel dropped her bouquet and it thumped down the chapel steps. Groomsmen drew guns. Rose petals floated in the air.

Gray grabbed her by the elbow. "Natalie, move."

She stared at his face, a mask of calm. In his other hand, he held a gun.

Oh, God, this was really happening.

They'd prepared for it, planned for it. But to her, the possibility of someone shooting up her brother's wedding had never seemed real. More like a game of pretend her big brothers played as kids, with her too young to really contribute but valiantly trying to play along.

Her family. Oh, God.

At the top of the stairs, Ash pushed Rachel

back inside the church. Natalie couldn't see where Jolie had gone or Devin or her aunt and uncle. A woman she didn't know grabbed the flower girl and raced for cover behind a hedge.

"Come on, Natalie." Gray half picked her up, half pushed her.

She forced her feet to move, willed her legs to carry her where Gray was leading.

In moments, the area around the church steps cleared. Guests continued to scream. Men barked orders. Car doors slammed and engines roared to life.

Gray pushed through the gate and pulled her into the graveyard. Still holding her elbow, his grip firm as a vise, he steered her down a cobblestone walk that flanked the church.

Natalie's pulse throbbed in her ears. Her heel sank into a space between the stones. She stumbled forward and Gray caught her.

The church's wood siding splintered a foot from her head.

Gray bit out a curse. He released her, and both of them fell to the ground.

Natalie hit the stone path. Pain slammed through her hands and knees. Her ankle turned and she felt her heel snap.

Another shot hit a nearby tree.

"Behind the tombstone. Now!" Gray crawled for the closest stone, still grasping Natalie's arm, pulling her with him.

She pointed her toe, letting her broken shoe slip off, leaving it behind. Wet grass squished under her knees. Her dress tangled around her legs. She couldn't breathe fast enough, couldn't scoop in enough oxygen to fill her hungry lungs.

They reached a patch of mud and kept crawling. A wide monument of red granite loomed ahead, spanning two or more graves. Gray pressed her up against the cold stone and covered her with his body.

She panted, trying to think, trying to breathe. The full impact of what had just happened slammed into her, making her dizzy. All the guests, some of them children. What kind of monster shot into a crowd filled with children?

"Is anyone hit? Did you see if anyone was shot?" She tried to raise her head, to look around, but she couldn't move.

Gray's chest was a solid wall behind her back. He splayed one hand on the crown of her head, preventing her from moving. "You have to keep your head down. Whoever this is, he's gunning for you, Natalie. Stay down."

Gray didn't understand. This wasn't just

about her. Not this time. "He was shooting into the crowd."

"But after the crowd broke, he kept gunning for you. He knows where we crawled. He might still be watching us through his sights right now."

She moved her head in a nod. She realized that. Yes. Gray was right. She had to keep her head down. The bullet that splintered the chapel's siding was meant for her, as was the one that hit the tree. She could absorb that much. What she couldn't fathom was the fact that he'd shot into the crowd. That innocent people who couldn't possibly have anything to do with this man could have died. They could be lying on the pavement dying right now. "Did anyone get shot?" Her voice sounded strangled in her own ears.

"I didn't see anyone go down." His voice was gentler, though still commanding.

"But you don't know. I don't want anyone hurt because of me. I…"

"Listen, Natalie." He spoke into her ear, his breath warm against her cheek and neck. "I didn't see anyone get hit. But even if someone was, *you* can't do anything about it. You rush out there, and you're dead. That crowd was half made up of cops. They have the training to deal with this. They know how to handle situations like this better than you do. They'll make sure everyone's safe."

She knew he was right. "I just—"

"You just nothing. The shooter is tracking *you*. He's waiting to get an angle on *you*. If you go back to the front of the chapel, you'll be putting everyone else in danger."

A sob lodged thick in her throat. He was right. Of course, he was right. Ash and his fellow officers could handle the crowd. Anyone around her was in danger. Someone was trying to kill her. If she didn't want to truly accept that after the push into the street and the shooting at Gray's apartment, she had no choice but to accept it now.

Her heart was beating so hard, she felt dizzy and nauseous. She pulled in a shuddering breath and struggled to find some amount of calm. "What do we do next?"

"We find a way out of here."

"How?" She didn't know if panic had short-circuited her brain or what, but she couldn't seem to think. And she had no idea how they would ever get out of this.

"We wait."

"Wait?"

"He knows right where we're hiding. As soon as we move out from behind this tombstone, he'll get his shot."

So they were trapped? "Where is he?"

"As far as I can tell, he has to be some-where in those buildings across the street. Probably an upper floor. The longer we make him wait, the better odds the police have of finding him."

Sirens screamed, the sound echoing through city streets.

"So he'll either wait and get caught or run."

She could feel Gray's nod. "That's his choice."

Everything he said made sense. At the same time, every nerve in her body was still screaming to run. She stayed still, trusting Gray.

More sirens joined the cacophony, the cav-alry on its way.

"See? He can't afford to stay there much longer."

Relief trembled through Natalie's body.

Gray shuffled behind her. Before she could tell what he was doing, he draped his jacket over her bare arms and shoulders.

She realized tears were streaming down her face, but she didn't wipe them away. She just focused on the heat of Gray's body. The scent of him, so clean and masculine, wrapped around her like his embrace. "Thank you."

"For what?"

"Being here."

"I'll always be here when you need me."

As much as she longed to take his promise at face value, she knew she couldn't. He would be there while he was working as her bodyguard. But always?

"Tell you what..." He slipped his hand along her body, dug into the interior pocket of his tux jacket and pulled out his phone. Shifting so he sat slightly to the side of her, he tapped in a number and held it to his ear.

"Who are you calling?"

"Ash."

He held a one-sided conversation Natalie could only guess at, but by the time he cut off the call, she was feeling a little calmer. She waited for Gray to report what her brother had said.

"First, no one was hit."

Natalie shifted her hip against the tombstone and slumped against the cold granite. "Thank God."

"But they didn't find the shooter yet. They're still searching."

"So what do we do?"

"There's no way he's still set up in that building. By now, he's probably gone. He would have been seen. So I'm taking you out of here."

She braced her hands on the stone, ready to push herself up.

He held up a hand. "In a few seconds."

"What happens until then?"

He gestured for her to wait. Then before she realized what he was going to do, he stood up.

Natalie cried out. She caught his fingers and tried to pull him down.

He stood for a few long seconds, then crouched back beside her.

Anger swept over her, fluctuating from cold to hot. "What were you doing?"

"Testing the water."

"You were trying to draw his fire." She wanted to hit him, wanted to pound her fists against his chest. "Why did you do that?"

"To draw him out. I had to be sure he was gone, that he hadn't just changed positions before I let you move."

"You could have gotten killed."

He had the nerve to look her in the eye and nod. "Instead of you getting killed. It is my job, Natalie."

She shook her head. Her whole body trembled. She wanted to scream. She wanted to cry. "Getting killed is not your job."

"If it saves you, it is."

Tears filled her eyes, and she couldn't stop them. She didn't know if it was facing the fact that Gray could have died or that he was willing to lay down his life for her that hit her hardest. Unable to sort one feeling from another, she covered her face in her hands. Leaning against the headstone, she let the sobs sweep her away.

A LOW MIST SETTLED over the graveyard as twilight approached. Red-and-blue lights swirled outside the front of the chapel, and voices rumbled through the dim haze.

When Ash finally called with the go-ahead, Gray holstered his weapon and lifted Natalie into his arms. She circled his neck with her arms and held on, one foot dangling bare. She had stopped crying by then, but neither of them said a word.

She felt light in his arms, fragile. When he thought about how close she had come to getting hurt, not once but three times, it made him break out in a sweat. And after witnessing her fear and tears, it was obvious that the past couple of weeks had taken its toll.

He needed to take care of her, and the sooner he could get her someplace safe, the better.

Gray carried Natalie into the chapel where the Kendall family had gathered along with many of the other guests. They exchanged relieved hugs as officers took statements. Gray let her out of his sight only once, leaving her discussing plans with her aunt, uncle and brothers as he described his version of events to law enforcement.

As he returned to the nave to collect Natalie, Devin clapped him on the shoulder. "Thank you. I know I was hard on you before, but..."

Gray waved away the rest. He didn't need apologies. Not when everything Devin had ever criticized him for had been spot-on.

The moment he reentered the nave, Natalie's eyes locked on his. She looked tired, her makeup smudged from crying, her dress covered in mud. Nasty bruises marred her knees. She padded to him, feet bare. "Rachel and Ash are calling off the reception."

"Of course." He'd never considered them going ahead with the postwedding party. Not in light of what had taken place.

"We have all these rooms at the hotel. We were all going to stay there after the reception."

A hotel sounded like a good idea. But judging by the implications of Natalie's words and tone, she didn't agree. "And those plans have changed?"

"My aunt and uncle are going to stay. I don't know about my brothers. But I just want to go home. Do you think that would be a problem? Devin said he has arranged for two security guards to be posted at the estate grounds all night anyway, and Ash promised police would drive by often."

As much as he preferred the hotel idea, Gray found himself nodding. After all Natalie had been through, if she wanted to spend the night in her own bed, he was not going to deny her. "I think with three of us and police backup, you'll be the safest woman in St. Louis."

She gave him a smile.

"Do you want to go?"

"Please."

She fetched her street clothes from the church office, slipped on her sneakers and coat and said her goodbyes. Outside, two uniformed officers circled outside the cemetery fence, walking along the street where Gray's car was parked. After a few words with a lieutenant at the scene, confirming none of the guests had been seriously hurt, they were finally on their way.

Twice on the way back to the Kendall

Estate, Gray noticed cars following. He turned off, taking circuitous routes. Both times, his paranoia was just that. Paranoia. By the time they wound through the gardens and spotted Natalie's house, he was pretty sure both of them were totally wrung out.

They entered the house. While she showered, he peeled off his now-ruined tuxedo and pulled on jeans and an old flannel shirt. He doubted there would be much sleep for him. What he'd told Natalie at the chapel had been true. He really didn't see any lone gunman making it past the two guards in the grounds and him. Hell, after today, the police would probably be looking over the place every ten minutes, as well. But it wasn't fear that threatened to keep him awake. It was concern for Natalie.

He'd never been good at dealing with emotions, but Natalie's crying jag in the cemetery had particularly scared him. Life-and-death stress like that was hard for special forces to take. For a civilian, it could be devastating.

He heated water and found the tea bags right where Natalie's aunt said they'd be. He'd just filled a cup and plopped in a tea bag when Natalie emerged.

She padded out of the bedroom hallway wrapped in a fluffy robe. Her hair was dry and pinned up on top of her head. Her cheeks were rosy, a nice contrast from the stark paleness of her skin earlier.

He carried the steaming cup from the kitchen and met her in the living room. "I have some tea for you."

She raised her brows. "Oh, please, tell me it's not chamomile."

"I hear it helps you sleep." The slightly dry grassy smell wafted toward him on the steam.

"You're worried about me having nightmares after today?"

He had to admit, it had crossed his mind.

She wrinkled her nose. "If I have to drink that stuff, I can guarantee nightmares."

"Don't like chamomile, eh?"

"I just don't have the nerve to break it to my aunt Angela." She crossed to bookshelves lining one wall and took a decanter down from one shelf. "How about scotch instead?"

He set the cup down. "Now you're talking."

She carried the booze to the kitchen, pulled out two tumblers and poured two fingers in each. Then they sat on the couch and sipped their whiskey.

The heat of the alcohol seared Gray's throat and warmed his head. Slowly he felt the tension of the past two weeks unfurl from his muscles.

He couldn't afford to have more than one drink. Natalie was safe with the men outside, but he wasn't about to take any chances. Still, this was precisely what he needed. He hoped it was everything she needed, as well.

He eyed her, sitting a foot away on the couch, staring at the blank television screen. She'd been quiet since she'd poured their drinks and she had begun to worry her lower lip between her teeth.

"What are you thinking?" he said.

"Honestly?"

He nodded. He knew it could be dangerous to ask a woman that question, but he really wanted to know. And it was better she voice her concerns to him than dream about them tonight.

"I was just going over why you stood up in the graveyard, why you risked your life like that."

"As I said, it's my job."

She shook her head, having none of it. "You say you regret your friend dying, that you feel you should have been able to save him."

The warmth in his bloodstream turned to cold and his head started to ache. When he'd asked, he'd been trying to help her. He didn't much like the spotlight to be turned on him.

Natalie watched him carefully and went on. "But that's only part of it. You wish it was you who died in Yemen. You wish you had been killed instead of him, don't you?"

Did he? Of course, he did. Not that Natalie could understand. "You don't know—"

"Don't give me that. I could have saved my parents. One scream and they never would have died."

He nodded, remembering word for painful word each thing she'd told him days ago in the basilica. "But you were six years old. And you don't know that you could have saved them. If it was the killer who came into your room that night, he might have visited you after they were already dead."

She stared down at the tumbler in her hands. It took her a moment, but she finally looked back up into his eyes. "You couldn't have controlled your situation any more than I could. Could you?"

Could he? He didn't know. But he should have. "I should have seen the risk of the charges going off. I should have taken them myself."

"Why? Your friend was doing his job, same as you."

He shook his head. He didn't expect her to understand. "Jimbo, he had a wife."

"So that makes you worth less?"

He shook his head. She didn't understand. How could she? "I promised her I'd watch over him, that I'd bring him back to her. I always came through before. With everything in my life, I've always come through." His throat tightened. A weight bore down on his chest. "But not that day. That day, I failed."

"Have you talked to her? Since it happened?"

"Yes." He didn't want to think about the memorial service, let alone the other night outside the coffee shop. Sherry's words were burned into his mind. He'd never forget them. Never forget the pain in her eyes. Never forget the look of betrayal and contempt.

"It didn't go well, I take it."

"You could say that."

"She blames you?" Natalie set her glass on the coffee table and folded her hands between her knees.

He wasn't sure how to explain it to her. None of it was simple. None of it was easy. "I've never had to sacrifice to get what I want, not like she and Jimbo did, even before his death."

"And that's why you think he's a better man?"

"He *was* a better man." Of that he had no doubt.

"Obviously, I didn't know him. But if you admire him that much, that says he was pretty special."

Gray nodded, and he took a sip of scotch. He didn't know what else to say. He didn't even know if his voice would function.

"I don't know Sherry, either. And I don't know what happened in Yemen. But for what it's worth, I think you're a very special man."

He shook his head and looked away. He couldn't say her statement didn't feel good. It felt better than good. But he wasn't sure he could bring himself to believe it.

She slipped her hands free and shifted closer to him. She raised her fingers to his jaw, stroking his cheek, and turned his head back to face her. "I'm not saying that to be nice. I mean it with all my heart."

Shivers fanned over his skin, starting at her fingertips and moving outward like ripples in a pond. He skimmed his knuckles down the silky blond length of her hair. He didn't know if he was ready to absorb the idea that she cared for him. He couldn't quite digest it. But the surge of feeling he had in answer was no surprise. "I appreciate the thought. Really. But no matter how special you think I am, it can't be half as special as you are."

Her lips parted. She tilted her face up to him.

He didn't know if he deserved it or believed it, all he knew was he couldn't stop himself. He brought his lips to hers.

She tasted sweet, and warmth moved through him just as it had when he'd first sipped the whiskey. He kissed her lightly, grazing her lips with his, teasing her with his tongue. Then he gathered her closer and delved deep.

She looped her arms around him. Her breasts pressed against his chest under the soft terry cloth. Her hair fell over his arms, soft as silk.

He breathed in the light floral scent of soap and something so much sweeter beneath. He skimmed his hand under her robe and touched smooth skin. The last time he'd touched her like this, he'd known it was wrong. That she didn't know the real him. That she wouldn't accept him if she'd known the truth.

Now every movement, every sensation, felt natural. As if he couldn't do anything else. As if he shouldn't even try.

She shrugged the robe from her shoulders. She was naked underneath, and in the back of his mind, he wondered if she'd hoped for this all along. Longed for it as much as he did.

He cupped her breasts in his hands and found her nipples with his fingers. He massaged and kneaded, and suckled them with his mouth.

She arched her back, pushing into him, asking for more. A moan vibrated low in her chest, and he thought it was probably the sexiest thing he'd ever heard. When he returned his lips to hers, she clawed at his shirt, opening buttons, discarding it on the floor.

He held her skin to his and kissed her deep. He didn't know how long they kissed like that. Time seemed to blur. Thoughts seemed to fade until there was only her. Only them.

She lowered her hand to his waist and unbuttoned his jeans. The denim was tight, his erection stretching the fabric to its limit. She lowered the zipper.

He stood. This time he didn't bother to divest himself of the jeans first then the briefs. He pushed them all down his legs at once, eager to be naked, wanting to be as close to her as he could get.

He paused for a moment and just drank in the sight of her sitting on the couch naked and flushed. He'd seen her naked before, and still the beauty of her body, the perfect shape of her breasts, the trim V between those long, long legs...he was struck all over again.

She moved her own gaze over his chest, his belly and down to his cock. And when she smiled, he felt like a damn superhero.

He had no idea if he deserved this woman, but he wanted to. He wanted to make love to her at night and wake in the morning with her wrapped in his arms. He wanted to bask in her smile and make her the most important part of every day. He wanted her to be proud of him. He wanted to give her everything.

He knelt down on the carpet.

She leaned forward, and he claimed her mouth. He littered kisses down her neck and over her collarbone. He suckled her nipples and devoured her scent.

Nudging her knees apart, he slipped his body between them and fitted his mouth to her most intimate place.

She tasted fine and clean. He moved against her, thrust his tongue into her. And when her moans built until she cried out his name, he knew he had to hear more of that glorious sound.

Their night had only begun.

Chapter Fourteen

When Natalie woke, she was sore. Muscles she hadn't even realized she had ached. And she knew she had Gray to thank.

He lay on his back next to her, one arm cupping her shoulder, the other cradling her to his chest. Last night, he'd made her feel things she never had before. Not just sexual pleasure, although there was plenty of that. But deeper satisfaction. He not only had a talent for protecting her, he made her feel strong all on her own.

She could stay in this bed, in his arms, all day and still not want to leave by nightfall. She nuzzled his neck, and his arms tightened around her.

"Umm, ready for more?" He peered at her through one open eye.

She giggled like a woman who was in love.

Her heart stilled. She couldn't keep a smile from spreading over her lips. A woman in love. That was what she was. As much as she hadn't wanted to admit it, deep down she'd known she was falling for Gray Scott for a long time. Maybe since they'd met. But it was only now she could let the thought fully bloom in her mind.

Last night, he'd made her feel so loved. So strong. So secure with the world. She wanted that feeling forever. And she wanted this man in her bed for the rest of her life.

"What is that smile for?"

A jitter seated itself somewhere between her stomach and her chest. She wanted to tell him. She wanted to tell everyone she knew. She wanted to scream it to the world.

"Is it a secret?"

"I suppose." Not exactly as bold as she'd been feeling. But it was the best she could do. After she'd discovered Gray was her bodyguard, she'd planned to hold off on investing her feelings until she could see if he would leave when his job was over. Obviously after last night, his job was far from over. Also, after last night, she'd already invested her mind, heart and soul.

"Can I guess what it is?" His hazel eyes sparked green among brown, like trees sprouting in spring.

She propped herself up on one elbow. The

sheet fell away from her body and exposed her bare breast.

His eyes flicked down her body. Raising his hand, he brushed her nipple with a finger until it was stiff with want.

A breath shuddered from her chest.

He grinned. "So, can I make a guess?"

She swallowed into a dry throat. In a perfect world, he would guess what she was feeling. He would swear he was falling in love with her, too. He would promise to never leave. "You can try."

He pressed his lips together and rolled them in toward his teeth. "You are thinking of what we did last night, and you're hoping I'll be up for more this morning."

She laughed. It wasn't that she wasn't thinking that. How could she not? But she was a little disappointed he hadn't professed his undying love all the same.

So much for her perfect world. Good thing this one was pretty close. "Care to try again?"

He sat up on his pillows and put his arms behind his head. His body stretched long and lean on the bed. The sheet slipped down, exposing his muscular arms, broad chest and six-pack abs.

She traced the line of his scars with her eyes, scars she'd kissed and licked last night, as if by her kiss, she could heal them. She could only hope that would be true, with time. And that he could heal hers, as well.

"Hmm." He hummed, the sound rumbling in his chest. "I got it. You want to try something totally different? Out in the garden? Swinging from a tree?"

She smiled and focused on his eyes. "Last night meant a lot to me, Gray." Her voice was barely a whisper, and she hadn't really said all she wanted to, but she still felt a jolt from exposing herself so much. A jolt, and then a surge of power.

He swallowed, his Adam's apple moving smoothly up and down. "It meant a lot to me, too, Natalie. More than you could ever know."

She leaned down and kissed him, her hair falling around them like a curtain, cutting them off from the world. They kissed for a long while. Finally Natalie sat up straight, the sheet slipping totally off her body.

Gray's gaze roamed over her breasts and down between her legs. Everywhere his eyes touched, she felt hot as fire. He circled one nipple with a finger, then trailed it down between her legs. "Is this what you had in mind?" He pushed back the sheet. He was ready for her, as hard as he had been last night.

She glanced away from him just long enough to get a glimpse of the clock. "We have to get ready for brunch."

His eyebrows shot upward. "Brunch?"

"Ash and Rachel are opening their gifts this morning."

He moved his hand between her thighs. "And we can't skip it? Or at least be a little late?"

She stifled a moan. "You still haven't guessed what I was thinking."

"Please say you weren't thinking of brunch."

She shook her head, his motions and the sensations they were causing making it difficult to speak.

"Okay, then you got me. What was it?"

"I was thinking that if we shower together, we might save a little time. And water."

His grin spread over his lips and sparkled in his eyes. "Oh, yes, I like how you think."

WATCHING NATALIE WALK buck naked to the bathroom, Gray had to smile. She was truly gorgeous, and so sexy, it made him hot all over again looking at her, not that he'd cooled yet.

Far from it.

But as hot as she was, he had to admit it was more than physical beauty with Natalie. She had a generous heart, a good soul. She made him feel stronger than he had with any other woman he'd ever known. Strong and good. Like he could do anything.

He had no earthly clue how he'd gotten so lucky. All the fortunate circumstances of his life—the affluent parents, his physical gifts, the purpose he'd found in the military—all of it paled in comparison to this woman and the fact that she cared for him.

From the bathroom, he could hear the water of the shower hiss to life.

He sat up and threw the covers back. He was ready for her still. He seemed to be ready all night. And if she'd have him, he was pretty sure he'd be ready for the rest of his life.

The doorbell chimed through the cottage.

Great. He levered himself up from the bed. So much for his hopes of joining Natalie in the shower. He strode to the living room, dug his robe out of his suitcase and threw it on. Then he strode to the front door and peered through the monitor window.

Natalie's brother Ash stood outside.

A small jolt of adrenaline spiked Gray's

bloodstream. He opened the door. "I thought we were going to the hotel for brunch. And aren't you supposed to be starting your honeymoon?"

"Police work doesn't always wait for brunch. Or for honeymoons." Ash walked into the living room. He appeared to take in the surroundings casually, but Gray could see what he was doing. A once-over of the living room stalled at the couch, the couch on which no one had slept last night. He cocked his head as if listening for something, then turned back to Gray. "Natalie?"

"In the shower."

Again, he eyed Gray and the empty couch. "Sleep well?"

"Yes." Gray braced himself for the brotherly warning that was sure to follow.

But instead of launching into a protective diatribe à la Devin, Ash gave a businesslike nod. "We have pushed the brunch gift opening thing back to dinner. We have a lead."

"Something on the shooter?"

"Possibly."

"What is it?"

Ash stepped past Gray and into the room. "You might want to sit down."

Sit down? Gray shook his head. How did that make sense? Was he trying to protect his sister? Keep her from getting upset? "Natalie is in the shower. She can't hear us."

"I'm not concerned about Natalie." He shrugged. "Well, not any more concerned than usual. This morning, I'm concerned about you."

"Me?" Again he shook his head, as if rearranging the brains inside would help make sense of the detective's strange comments.

"They received this at the Kendall Communications office." He pulled out a sheet of paper and handed it to Gray.

The printout of an email. Gray skimmed the page. And as he took in the name of the sender, his gut ached as if he'd been punched.

The image of the person in the light blue sweatshirt flitted through his mind. The shooting at his apartment. The sniper at the wedding. He'd been wrong about all of it. So wrong. Natalie might have been the target, but only to get at him.

How could he have let this happen? How did he not see where the threat was coming from? How could he have been so deaf and blind?

He looked up at Ash. "Have you found her?"

"We're looking for her now."

"I can give you a list of people she knows."

Ash nodded. "That would be helpful."

He knew there was more that he had to do. More that he couldn't put off, no matter how much it hurt. "And tell Devin he needs to hire a replacement. Natalie must be protected, and I can't put her in danger anymore."

NATALIE TURNED OFF the shower and grabbed a towel from the bathroom rack. When she'd stepped under the warm spray, she'd been expecting Gray to join her. He never had. Finally now that her skin was starting to prune, she couldn't wait anymore. She needed to find out why.

She dried her body and wrapped the towel around her hair in a turban. Last night had been amazing, and to wake in Gray's arms this morning and hear him tell her last night had meant so much to him, as much as it had to her...that had been even better. There could be countless reasons he hadn't made it into the shower. A myriad of things might have come up. She needn't feel uneasy.

So why did she?

She paused at the door. It was still open a few inches, just as she'd left it when she'd jumped under the hot spray. She could detect no sounds from the master bedroom. Bracing herself, she pulled the bathroom door open wide. The bedroom was empty. Gray's clothes were gone from the floor. There was no sign of Gray ever having been there, except that the bed was made.

The tremor in her stomach had nothing to do with the fact that she hadn't had breakfast. She hurried into the closet, selected a pair of jeans and a sweater and pulled them on. She rushed back into the bathroom. After untwisting the towel, she ran a comb through her hair and left it to air-dry.

She had to find Gray.

She tried to push away the irrational fear beating at the back of her mind. He wouldn't just leave. He couldn't. Not after she'd opened her heart to him. Not after all they'd shared.

She rushed out to the living room.

Gray stood in the kitchen, a cup of coffee in his hand, staring out the window above the sink. He was wearing the same jeans he'd changed into last night, and a long-sleeved T-shirt stretched across his broad shoulders.

He hadn't left.

Natalie's knees felt shaky with relief. She pulled in a breath, trying to steady herself. She had no reason to fear. None at all. She needed to keep calm. She pushed a lilt into her tone. "Decided not to take a shower?"

He turned to face her. Lines etched his

forehead and bracketed his mouth. He looked more serious and worried than Natalie had ever seen him. "Coffee?" He turned back to pour her a cup.

"What happened?" Natalie wasn't sure she wanted to know, but she forced the words out anyway. "Was someone hurt?"

"No one was hurt. It's not that." He crossed the kitchen and handed her the cup.

"Thank God." She wrapped her fingers around the warm ceramic mug and breathed in the rich scent. At least she didn't have to worry that yesterday's gunman had done something horrible to someone she loved. But as relieved as she was, she suspected she wasn't going to like whatever Gray had to say. And she had a feeling the warmth and belonging and joy she'd felt last night and this morning were at an end. "So tell me."

"Your brother Ash stopped by."

"Ash?" She could just imagine her brother finding Gray half-dressed, figuring out what had happened between her and Gray and making some kind of attempt to protect her heart. "Did he say something to you? About me? About us?"

"I think he knows I spent the night in your room last night, but no. That's not why he was here."

Her throat felt dry. She tried to swallow, but it was no use. "Then why?"

"They got a lead on the shooter."

"But that's fantastic." There had to be something he wasn't telling her, something he was hesitant to say. "Why is that not fantastic?"

"It is fantastic."

"You don't look like it is."

"It's not that this isn't a good development. I'm just…" He pulled out a piece of paper and offered it to her. "This was sent to Kendall Communications."

She took the sheet. It looked like a printout of an email. The paper rattled in her trembling hand. Scooping in a fortifying breath, she read.

Dear Kendall Communications,

I am writing to warn you about a man who is working for you. His name is Grayson Scott, and he is not only a liar, but a war criminal. He has proven selfish and dangerous in the past. He is also a murderer who brutally caused my husband's death.

If you don't fire Grayson Scott immediately, I will have no choice but to deal with him myself. And if any of you try to stop me or stand in the way, you will pay, too.

Natalie looked up from the paper and focused on Gray. The uneasy feeling she'd had when she'd first realized Gray wasn't joining her in the shower buzzed along every nerve. "Do they know who wrote it?"

"The police believe it's from Jimbo's wife. Jim Russel. The friend I told you about."

The friend who had died in Yemen.

She looked back down at the email and read it again, but she still couldn't make it turn out any differently than the first time. "It doesn't make a lot of sense."

"She blames me. She might want to hurt you to get back at me for Jimbo's death."

She'd gotten that much. The rest shuffled into place when she looked into Gray's eyes. "So the person who pushed me into traffic, the one who shot up your apartment, the sniper at Ash and Rachel's wedding, all those were her?"

"It looks like it, yes."

She could see where this was going. Gray was blaming himself. Just as he had blamed himself for his friend's death, he was now blaming himself for putting her and her family in danger. "She must be very troubled."

He pressed his lips into a bloodless line and said nothing.

She reached out and laid a hand on his arm. "You know this isn't your fault, either."

Circles dug under his eyes, not from lack of sleep but from stress. "You could have been killed, Natalie."

"But that's not because of you."

"Who is it because of?"

"Sherry. If she's really the one running around shooting at people, it's Sherry's fault. Sherry's actions. You're not responsible for the things she chooses to do."

He shook his head. "She hasn't been stable since Jimbo died. She's had emotional problems. A nervous breakdown. I don't know what else."

She wasn't getting through to him. That was obvious. He'd stacked up years of guilt and self-blame and an annoying habit of taking responsibility for everything and everybody. She had to find some way to get him to listen. She had last night. Maybe she could break through his walls again. "You told me I couldn't blame myself for not screaming the night my parents died."

"We've been over that, Natalie. It isn't the

same." He pulled his arm away from her touch and paced the length of the living room floor. "Here your brother hired me to be your bodyguard, and yet you would have been far safer if he'd never called. By just being here, being around you, I've put you in danger."

She shook her head. She wanted to touch him, hold him. She needed to make him see. "But you couldn't have known that."

"I should have. I saw Sherry."

"When?"

"That night we first met, I went back to the coffee shop to ask the barista about your admirer. Sherry was waiting for me outside. She threatened to make me regret breaking my promise and letting her husband sacrifice his life for me. She must have followed me, saw I was protecting you."

"That was the night my house was broken into and vandalized."

He nodded. "That was the night it all started. I was following you for weeks before that. There was no sign of any danger. That's because Sherry didn't know about your connection to me until then. I brought the danger down on you that night."

She clawed her wet hair back from her face. She had to convince him to listen, but how? She was so frustrated, she could hardly breathe. "I'm getting the feeling I could repeat that it wasn't your fault for the rest of my life, and you would never believe it."

He crossed to the bay window overlooking the cottage's front gardens.

She followed him, stopping about ten feet behind. They were quite a pair, weren't they? Both crippled. Both unable to see beyond the prisons they'd built for themselves, constructed from their own guilt and blame. "I get it. I know how you feel. And I've done the same thing with my parents' murders. But I'll make you a promise. If you at least try to let this go, I'll do the same."

He turned away from the window, grabbed his jacket from the back of the couch and put it on.

Natalie watched him, no clue what to say or do. For the first time, she noticed the couch where, except for last night, Gray had been camping out since his apartment had been shot up and he'd confessed he was her bodyguard. The pillows were neatly arranged. The blankets he'd been using were nowhere to be seen.

And the small suitcase he'd brought from his apartment was gone. "Where are you going?"

"To the police station. Ash and the rest of

the P.D. are out trying to find Sherry right now. I want to be there in case they're successful."

"I'll get my coat and bag."

"No, Natalie. You need to stay here. I've asked Devin to hire another bodyguard. He just arrived."

"What?"

He motioned out the front window at a hefty hulk of a man striding up to the cottage. "If I'm Sherry's target, I need to stay away from you. That's the only way you'll be safe."

Natalie felt sick. After last night, she hadn't seen this coming. She'd really thought what she'd found with Gray was different. Maybe even permanent. Obviously it was all wishful thinking. "You're leaving."

"I'm sorry."

She could cry, she could plead with him not to go, she could grab him and kiss him and attempt to seduce him into staying. But it was no use. She felt bone tired, like she could curl up and sleep for weeks.

If he wanted to leave, he would. Nothing she could say or do would change it. "I'm sorry, too."

Chapter Fifteen

The police station seemed busy for a Sunday, not that Gray visited regularly enough to know. When the officer manning the entrance ushered him into a tiny, vacant room holding a table and two chairs bolted to the floor, Gray was more relieved to be by himself than unnerved by the camera peering down at him from the corner. The room smelled like body odor mixed with some kind of minty aftershave, but at least it was quiet enough to think.

Not that he relished more time to dwell on what he'd done to Natalie.

He'd hurt her when he'd left. Hurt her so badly, he doubted she would ever be able to forgive him, even when this was over. The look of abandonment in her eyes would haunt him forever. But he couldn't change it. He'd only wanted to do his job, to keep her safe. He couldn't let his feelings for her and his selfish need to be near her interfere with her safety. He had come close enough to making that mistake already.

The sound of knuckles rapping wood came from the door behind him. As he looked up, the door swung wide and Ash stepped into the room.

Gray shot up from his chair. "Well? Did you find her?"

"Yes." Ash's face looked drawn.

A bad feeling worked its way up Gray's spine and pinched at the back of his neck. He couldn't help fearing the worst. "Is she alive?"

"Yes."

He let out the breath he'd been holding. He just wished Ash would come out with it instead of making him ask for every crumb of information. "Is she here?"

Ash raked a hand through his hair. "She's not the one trying to kill Natalie."

No, she hadn't been trying to kill Natalie. He knew that already. If anything, she had intended to hurt Natalie to get at him. But he knew what was more likely to be her end-game. "She was trying to kill me."

Ash shook his head. "No. She has a lot of resentment aimed at you. That's obvious from her email to Kendall Communications.

But Sherry Russel wasn't the shooter. Not at your apartment and not at the wedding."

Gray shook his head. When Ash had showed him the email from Sherry, it had all added up. It had all made sense. He couldn't quite wrap his mind around what Ash was trying to tell him now. "Why do you think that?"

"Don't think it. Know. We found her at a mental health hospital. She's been there since the night you ran into her, the night she sent the email, the night Natalie's cottage was vandalized."

"That's not possible."

"The hospital records back it up. She's been in and out since her husband's death. She had her third nervous breakdown that night."

"Triggered by seeing me."

Ash tilted his head in acknowledgment. "Seems like it. But whatever the cause, she wasn't trying to kill Natalie. Or you. She was in the hospital during the shootings. It couldn't have been her."

Gray's head spun. He wanted to tell Ash he was wrong, but he clearly couldn't argue with hospital records.

Ash shifted his feet on the floor. "I'm sorry I dragged you into this. If I hadn't needed some background in order to find her, I wouldn't have come to you until we determined whether she was a viable suspect."

Gray waved away the apology. It hadn't been Ash's fault. It had been his own. And now that the first thing he'd done when the going had gotten tough was the one thing Natalie had feared all along, he wasn't sure where to turn.

He swallowed into a dry throat. "Do you have any other leads? Any ideas about who the shooter really is?"

"Afraid not. We followed up on what you and Natalie discovered about Demetrius Jones. He has solid alibis for the shootings, as well. But I still think you two might have been on the right track with those suspicions. The shredded paintings might very well be the detail that breaks this case."

Gray hadn't known Natalie's brother long, but the police detective had always seemed confident, maybe even to the point of being cocky. He didn't seem that way now. Something was bothering Ash, something a lot deeper than running low on leads. And Gray had a feeling he could guess what he was getting at. "You think the attacks on Natalie might be related to your parents' murders?"

Ash flinched, ever so slightly, but he

didn't deny that was where his thoughts were leading.

"You're looking for...who?" He thought about what Natalie had told him had happened that night. "The real murderer?"

Again, Ash didn't answer. Not directly. "We're looking for someone older. Someone who might suspect the paintings mean Natalie is able to identify him."

"Someone who might have also committed The Christmas Eve Murders," Gray supplied, and Ash didn't correct him.

NATALIE LEANED CLOSE to the mirror. She was still trembling, making it difficult to sweep mascara on her lashes without stabbing herself in the eye. Not that an accident like that could make her eyes any more sore than they already were from crying.

She'd spent the morning trying to pull herself together. Finally she'd decided it was silly to knock around the cottage alone when she could simply show up at the hotel a little early and spend time with her family. If she could just lose herself in gift opening and wedding celebration, she wouldn't have to think about Gray leaving her.

Another surge of tears blurred her vision. How she could produce more, she didn't know. She abandoned the idea of mascara and walked to the living room.

Her bodyguard, a perfectly nice man named Chet, was watching a cable news channel on television. As she entered the room, he looked up. "Ready to go?"

She nodded and hoped she didn't look half the total mess she felt. "Whenever you are."

He pushed up from the couch. Tall and lean with plenty of muscle, Chet was the type of man Natalie was sure countless women swooned over. She half wished she could be one of them. It would be so much easier to fill the void Gray had left in her heart. Unfortunately she suspected no man would be able to do that for a long, long time. If ever.

He pulled on a dark blue jacket and held up a hand. "Let me bring the car around. I'll come back in and get you."

"You really think that's necessary? No one is really after me, as it turns out. All of this was about hurting someone else."

"My orders are to provide protection. You need to let me do my job."

She let out a sigh. Maybe she really was that hard to deal with. Obviously Devin thought so, otherwise he wouldn't have hired Gray to protect her on the sly. Now she was harassing poor Chet, when all he wanted was to do his job. "I'm sorry. It's been a tough weekend. I'll try not to take it out on you."

Chet gave her a smile that would melt most women's hearts. "Not a problem. Understandable. In this line of work, I usually see people when they aren't at their best. Now you wait. I'll come back in when I have the car ready and am sure the coast is clear."

She answered his smile the best she could. "Thanks, Chet."

He opened the front door. On the step outside, he paused. "Flip the dead bolt when I leave."

Natalie forced her eyes not to roll. Chet was doing his job and doing it well. He likely didn't know they'd already caught the shooter and now that Gray had walked out, Sherry no longer had reason to try to kill her. "Will do, Chet."

When the door closed behind him, Natalie did as he'd asked, locking the place up tight. Then, making herself pass by the couch where Gray had slept, without looking at it she wandered into the kitchen.

She took a few sips of cold coffee and cleaned up the countertops. When she'd finished, Chet still hadn't returned. She checked her watch. There was no way it would have taken him this long to get her car. She peered out the front bay window. The wind was still tossing trees and swirling dried leaves through the garden in mini tornadoes. Dark clouds scuttled across the blue sky, gathering in number. Her gaze rested on something dark between gold and white chrysanthemums and bushes of purple aster.

She shifted to one side of the window, trying to get a better look.

Natalie's heart stuttered.

The dark color was the deep blue of a jacket. And wearing that jacket, was a man. Chet. Facedown in the garden and not moving.

Chapter Sixteen

Gray loaded the heavy file box into the trunk of his car and climbed behind the wheel. He closed the door, grateful to get out of the wind. The weather's dark bluster seemed to reflect the turmoil inside him. He longed to go back to Natalie's house, to beg her to forgive him, to promise he'd never leave her again. But he couldn't put her through that. Not when leaving her might possibly have been the best gift he could have given her.

He never should have mixed his personal feelings with his duty. He should have learned that lesson in Yemen. All SEALs watch each other's backs, but Natalie was right last night when she said by promising Sherry that he would be Jimbo's protector, he'd upset the balance. He'd become Jimbo's protector instead of his fellow soldier. And as a result, he'd failed everyone involved.

And now he'd done the same thing with

Natalie. This morning, protecting her had meant walking away, loving her had meant staying. He'd been torn between the two, and as a result, he hadn't succeeded in accomplishing either.

At least now she had a bodyguard who had his head in the right place.

He slipped his key in the ignition and started the car. He knew what he had to do. He might not be on the Kendall payroll any longer, but that didn't mean he was going to give up protecting Natalie. And he was going to start by finding the bastard who was trying to kill her.

He'd start with the old case file Ash had let him copy. He'd hole up in his apartment and go through each interview, each report. He wasn't as good an investigator as a detective like Ash; he knew that. But maybe looking at the case with fresh eyes would help.

It certainly couldn't hurt.

He leaned forward, ready to shift the car into gear, and then paused. An uneasy feeling pinched the back of his neck. He rolled one shoulder then the other, but it did no good.

He fished in his jacket and pulled out his cell phone. He couldn't drop in on Natalie and check on her just to leave again. Not unless he wanted to prove Sherry was right about his selfishness and disregard for others. That's why, before he'd left, he'd gotten her new bodyguard's cell phone number.

He punched in the digits and held the device to his ear. Five rings later, he was switched to voice mail.

Damn.

He punched in the number again and got the same result. This time, he waited for the tone. "Chet, this is Gray Scott. I just wanted to check with you. Make sure everything's going okay and Natalie is safe. Call me back as soon as you get this. Please call. Right away." He left his number, even though Chet's phone should have a record of it, then cut the call.

He shifted into Drive and pulled out into traffic. Shoulders tight, he willed the phone to ring, for Chet to respond to his message, but the call never came. He'd driven about a mile in the direction of his apartment, when he finally gave in and turned around.

Chet Lawson might not be answering for a myriad of reasons. But that didn't mean Gray could leave a message and go on with his business. Above all, he had to know Natalie was okay.

To him, it was the only thing that mattered.

NATALIE'S HANDS SHOOK so badly, she dropped her cell phone. She picked it up off the carpet and managed to hit the numbers 911. She held it to her ear, a silent prayer racing through her mind.

Nothing.

No ringing, no dial tone, nothing—only static and the sound of her pulse drumming in her ears. She stared at the little screen. *No service.*

It couldn't be a coincidence. Someone was blocking the signal. They had to be.

Sherry?

She glanced out the window again, focusing on Chet's still form, then skimming the garden's bushes and wind-tossed trees.

She couldn't see anyone outside, but that didn't mean Sherry wasn't there. Natalie thought about yesterday, the bullet slamming into the church, just missing her head.

Was that what happened to Chet? Had he been shot? And if she stepped outside, if she made a run for it, what would stop her from being gunned down?

She moved away from the window. If Gray were here, that was the first thing he'd tell her. Stay away from windows. A thought shuddered into her mind.

If Gray were here, would he be the one lying out in the garden?

A strangled sound whimpered deep in her throat. She couldn't think that way. She had to make a plan. And in order to do that, she had to calm down.

She forced herself to breathe. In and out. In and out. She hadn't heard shots fired. She'd heard banging and other wind sounds, but no shots. Unless the sound had been suppressed in some way.

She didn't know what to do, but she didn't want to stay here and wait to die. Maybe she could risk running for it. Maybe she could get away. She didn't have to walk out the front door.

She grew up on this estate. She knew every inch of these gardens. Maybe she could go out the side door, cut through the shade and rose gardens and make it to the mansion to call for help before Sherry knew she was gone.

She grabbed her jacket. If her heart beat any harder, it would burst through her rib cage. She moved through the dinette and reached the side door. The thin, white curtain stretched over the glass inset from top to bottom, letting in light but obscuring the view. She hooked the fabric with a trembling finger and did her best to peer through the space. She could see nothing but bushes and trees tossing in the wind. The frying-pan size leaves of a hosta lily rocked back and forth like a small child soothing itself to sleep.

Here goes nothing.

She released the curtain and grabbed the doorknob. One, two, three. She scooped in a deep breath, twisted the knob and yanked.

The door didn't budge.

She yanked again. No movement.

Something crashed toward the back of the house.

A scream started to fill her throat. She choked it back along with a breath…a scent. She'd been an artist too long not to know that smell anywhere.

Paint thinner. And something else.

Smoke.

She pulled at the door, throwing her full weight behind the yank. No good.

"Oh, my God. Oh, my God."

It was only a smell, but it gained strength fast. She had to get out of here. She pushed away from the blocked door. Reaching the living room, she froze.

What should she do?

Sherry could still be in the front. Waiting.

As if confirming her fears, a loud crash hit

the front door. Not gunfire, something heavy thrown against the house.

Then she heard the crackle. Smoke drifted through the crack under the door.

The front of her house was on fire.

She turned in the direction of the bedrooms. The smoke was building right in front of her eyes, starting as a slight haze then getting thicker, denser with each step she took.

The fire alarm in the bedroom hall shrieked to life. A few seconds later, the living room unit joined in.

She couldn't get out the front door or the side, and if someone was in front of her house, running into the garage wouldn't get her very far, either.

The back of the house was her best bet. She could escape through the windows and disappear into the thick gardens and cove of evergreen trees.

The smoke grew thicker, building impossibly fast. She reached out a hand and dragged her fingertips along the wall to guide her way. By the time she reached her studio, her eyes stung and tears soaked her cheeks.

She twisted the knob and gave the door a shove. It flew open. A hot whoosh hit her full in the face. She threw her arms up, trying to shield her eyes.

Instead of finding a way out, she'd walked right into another raging fire.

Blinking her eyes, she tried to look for the window, for a way out. Instead, all she saw were the bright flames and curling canvases as the remaining paintings of her memories burned.

GRAY TURNED DOWN THE tree-lined street leading to the Kendall mansion and Natalie's cottage, pressing down harder on the accelerator. Something was wrong; he could feel it. Why had he wasted valuable time questioning his instincts? Why had it taken him so long to decide to check on Natalie?

He swung the wheel, shooting for the driveway of the Kendall Estate. His tires screeched. The back end fishtailed, nearly hitting the curb. By some miracle, he made the turn. He gunned the engine again, swerving down the narrow twisty road winding through the gardens.

The security guards who had been posted on the property last night were gone today. When Gray had left, he hadn't thought that would be a problem. He'd thought that as long as he wasn't around, Natalie wasn't in danger. But that was before Ash had learned Sherry couldn't be the shooter. Now he wished those guards were here. Now he wouldn't feel comfortable unless he had an army.

The gray stone mansion peered down at him, three stories high. He drove past. No one was home, the entire family still at the hotel getting ready for their dinner and gift opening celebration. Gray prayed that was where Natalie had gone, as well. That his inability to reach Chet was due to overloaded downtown cell phone usage. But he suspected it wasn't that simple.

He continued past the pool house and followed the curving drive into the Kendall Estate's twenty acres of gardens.

A sharp pop split the air. Cracks spider-webbed across his windshield.

His heart slammed in his chest. He'd been right. There was something wrong. Very wrong. He bit out a curse and kept driving. He couldn't see the cottage. Not yet. He had two more bends to navigate.

He swerved around the first. Borderline too fast. A second shot hit, jarring through the car. The end swung wide. The sickening crunch of metal and the shattering of glass filled his ears and rattled through his brain. He jerked forward against his seat belt, then slammed back against the seat. The car slid to a stop against the broad trunk of an old oak.

He pulled in breath after breath. He was okay. He could still move. At least nothing had hit the front end. At least the air bag hadn't gone off and trapped him in the car for precious seconds.

He unhitched his seat belt and drew his weapon. The side of the car closest to the cover of trees and other vegetation bent inward toward him. He reached across and tried to open it anyway, but it wouldn't budge.

He'd have to take the hard way.

He grasped the driver's door latch. Drawing in a deep breath as if ready to plunge under water, he pulled. At the same time, he put his weight behind the push.

The door swung open and he went straight to the ground. Holding his pistol in front of him, he crawled on his belly.

Another shot exploded near him. A bullet pinged off the pavement a foot away.

He kept moving the way he'd been trained. He had no choice. Stop and he was dead.

He made it to the other side of the car and dived into a cluster of bushes.

Branches scratched at his face and hands. Damn. Roses. Their thorns ripped into the leather of his jacket.

He tuned out the needlelike pricks and squinted in the wind. Judging from the trajectory of the gunfire, the shooter was somewhere between the mansion and Natalie's cottage, probably on the roof of the pool house.

He pulled out his cell phone. Since he hadn't realized his hunch was correct until turning onto the road leading to the estate, he hadn't tried to reach anyone other than Chet and Natalie. Now he wished he'd called 911 right away.

He punched in the three digits. No signal.

Damn. Whoever this shooter was, he was serious enough to have used a mobile cell phone jammer to interfere with reception. Unfortunately that meant Chet and Natalie could still be in the cottage and the jammer was preventing calls from going out and coming in.

He slipped the phone back into his pocket, wiped his sweaty right palm on his pants, then adjusted his grip on his gun. What he wouldn't give for an assault rifle about now. A 9mm Glock was nothing against the hardware this guy had. Probably the rifle he'd used to fire on the wedding and Gray's apartment.

He scanned the area, looking for areas of

vegetation he could use for cover. A scent reached him, the unmistakable smell of smoke riding on the wind.

No, no, no, no.

He squinted through the gardens in the direction of the cottage. From here he could only see one corner of the little house peeking through the trees. But along the tiny snatch of roofline was a white haze.

The cottage was on fire.

He detached himself from the rosebush. Keeping low, he half ran, half crawled through the gardens. He had to reach the cottage. It didn't take much imagination to guess the gunman's plan. Jam the phone signal and smoke Natalie and Chet into the open. Shoot them when they tried to escape the fire.

He prayed he wasn't too late to stop that from happening.

He moved into a grove of evergreen trees. Here the cover was thick enough for him to risk rising to his feet. He moved into a sprint. Wind howled through the trees, the branches' sway camouflaging his dash. Reaching the edge of the trees, he hunkered down behind a hedge that bordered the patch of yard and swooping lines of garden and cobblestone patio that flanked the cottage.

He could see the smoke clearly now.

Flames rose from the main entrance and licked outside the front door. Other wisps of gray seemed to be issuing from a broken pane on the side of the structure before swirling away in a squall. If he was judging the inside floor plan correctly, that set of windows belonged to the studio.

A sound came from behind him. He wasn't sure how he noticed it above the wind or why it stood out in his mind. But he'd been trained to react to threats, to depend on instinct and muscle memory.

He spun around, hands up.

A man lunged toward him, a small branch in his hands. Only about a foot and a half long and an inch in diameter, the stick didn't look like much, but Gray knew in the right hands, even a small, simple weapon like that could be deadly.

The man struck Gray across the stomach in a vicious circular motion. At the same time, he shifted his weight, putting the full force of it behind the blow.

Gray grunted, the breath whooshing from his lungs. His chin jutted forward in an involuntary movement. He brought his hands up, trying to block what he knew would come next.

Still gripping with both hands, the man

jabbed upward with the end of the stick, trying to drive it into Gray's neck, trying to kill him.

Gray brought his arm around, blocking the blow. The stick's point raked the side of his hand, drawing blood.

The man recovered quickly, trying to smash Gray across the face with the end of the stick.

Pain ripped across Gray's cheekbone. He staggered back, struggling to stay on his feet.

The attacker tried for a second blow, this time going for Gray's throat. Another shot aiming to render him unconscious or dead.

Gray was ready this time. He grabbed the stick. Twisting it with his right hand, he brought his left elbow hard into the guy's temple.

The blow jarred through his arm. Still gripping the stick, he struck again, then brought his knee up.

The man angled his body to the side, blocking the attack. He released the stick and came at Gray with an uppercut to the jaw.

The strike clanged through Gray's head. He counterstruck wildly, missing the target.

The attacker landed another bash to the side of his head.

Who was this guy? He was too young to be

the murderer of Natalie's parents. He was too trained to be a civilian. The only thing clear was that he was well versed in hand-to-hand combat. Gray had to end this before the guy ended him.

Gray seized the man's left arm with his right hand. Digging his fingers into the canvas jacket, he pulled downward. At the same time, he brought his right hand up, striking him under the chin with the heel of his hand. He gave a backward kick with his rigid left leg, throwing the guy to the ground.

He landed on his side, gasping for breath. Twisting his arm behind his back, Gray flipped him to his stomach and pinned him facedown in the evergreen needles and mulch. "Who are you?"

The guy sputtered and said nothing. He turned his head to the side, breathing heavily.

Gray stared at him. That face. He'd seen that face before. Not in real life, though. In a photograph. "You're Natalie's brother."

Again, the man remained silent.

"You're the news reporter. The third oldest. The one who's been overseas." Gray searched his memory for the name. "Thad, isn't it?"

"What the hell's going on here?"

Gray wished he could answer that one. He was still trying to put it together, and with his head still ringing from Thad's blows, thinking wasn't the easiest of tasks. He wiped the side of his face. His fingers came back coated with blood. "Man, where did you learn to fight like that?"

"Let me up."

Gray wasn't sure that was a good idea. Not until he and Thad reached an understanding. "That wasn't you shooting, was it?"

"It was you."

"No. I am Natalie's…I *was* Natalie's bodyguard."

"You're Gray."

He squinted down at the man. From everything Natalie said, the family had never gotten a hold of her third brother. The most they'd been able to do was leave a message. He wasn't sure how that added up to Thad knowing his name, but for now he'd just have to chalk it up to being part of a lot of things that weren't adding up about Thad. "Yes, I'm Gray Scott."

"Let me up, Gray, or I'll go back to trying to kill you."

Gray released his arm and took his weight off Thad's back. He held out a hand to help Natalie's brother to his feet.

Thad ignored the offer. He brushed evergreen needles and other debris from his face and clothing. "Where's Natalie?"

"I don't know. Dear God, she could be in the house." His own words sounded hollow and hopeless in his ears. "I have to get in there. I have to find her and get her out."

Thad narrowed his eyes, and Gray got the feeling he was being sized up. "You special forces?"

"Former SEAL."

"Sweet."

"You?"

"Reporter."

"Bull. No reporter fights like that."

Thad looked him straight in the eye. "I'm a foreign correspondent. I know how to defend myself."

Gray still didn't quite buy it, but they had no time to argue details. It would be tough to save Natalie and take down a gunman armed with an assault rifle all on his own. But with two of them, maybe they could be successful.

They had to be successful.

He scanned Thad's sides, looking for the bulge of a holster. "Are you armed?"

"If I was armed, do you think I'd attack you with nothing but a twig?"

Good point. "Here." Gray pulled the Glock

from his holster and handed it butt first to Thad.

"You have another?"

"No." He wished he did.

"Sure you don't want it?"

"You'll need it more."

Thad took the weapon, inspecting it as if he knew what he was doing. "How many in the clip?"

"Fifteen." There were clips that held more rounds, but they made a weapon heavy, awkward. Now Gray wished he'd accepted that trade-off. It would be nice to have twice as many bullets to work with. "Can you draw his fire? Give me a chance to get inside the house? Maybe give the neighbors enough reason to worry and call the cops?"

Thad nodded. "I'll do you one better. You save my sister, and I'll make sure the bastard comes nowhere near you."

Thad was a good fighter, but even so, Gray had his doubts. And if Thad was hurt in this, or killed…Gray shook his head. "I can't let you do that."

"What do you mean, let me? I thought we were working together in this. I don't need you to protect me. I need you to save my sister."

He was right. Gray hadn't trusted Jimbo to

do his job. Instead he'd tried to watch out for him, take care of him. As if he was the only one responsible. The only one who could do his duty and everyone else's.

He'd gone to the opposite extreme with Natalie. As soon as it seemed there was a conflict, he'd abandoned her altogether and left her with another bodyguard. As if he had to be responsible for everything or nothing, everyone or no one. As if that was the choice before him.

He focused on Thad. "You sure you can handle this?"

Natalie's brother stared back. He didn't look that much like his sister. He more closely resembled his brothers Devin and Ash. But similar features or no, he had that same Kendall determination Gray had witnessed shining in Natalie's eyes. "I can handle this," he said. "Trust me."

Gray nodded. He would. He did.

"Save my little sister. Do what it takes."

"I'll lay down my life for her," Gray whispered into the wind, but Thad was already gone.

Chapter Seventeen

Gray gave Thad a couple of seconds head start before he made his move. From here, he could hear the smoke alarms wail from inside the house. Gunfire erupted from the area near the swimming pool. Reports cracked out over the whistle of the wind, the flat pop of the pistol and the deeper, rounder timbre of the rifle.

Now.

Gray scooped in a deep breath and ran. As he emerged from cover, he half expected to hear bullets breaking the sound barrier around him, half expected to feel lead plowing into his back. He shoved the feelings aside. He had to concentrate on the mission. He had to focus on saving Natalie. And to do that, he first had to get into the cottage.

He raced across the area of lawn and vaulted low bushes and tall clusters of flowers. He came down on the patio, shoes skidding on cobblestone. Regaining his balance, he covered the rest of the distance to the side door that led into the dinette. He turned the doorknob and pushed.

It didn't budge.

He studied the frame. Long nails, like the spikes he'd found in the back of the cottage a week ago, had been driven through the wood and into the door itself. The shooter had nailed the door shut, and he'd obviously been planning this assault for some time.

Gray thought about the cottage's other entrances. He could try the front door, but he'd be exposing himself to the gunman once again, and judging from the burning pile on the front stoop, he might not be able to get in even if the door itself wasn't compromised.

He glanced along the side of the cottage. The bedroom windows were a possible entrance point, but they weren't very wide. He'd be lucky if he could squeeze his shoulders through. Same with the studio window, which was pouring smoke.

His gaze landed on a heavy wrought-iron planter at the corner of the patio. He made a step in the planter's direction.

The crack of a shot split the air. A round hit the cobblestone in front of him.

He fell back into the cover of the house.

Two pops came from deep in the gardens. Thad returning fire, drawing the shooter's attention.

Heart pounding in his ears, Gray kept low this time. Crouching forward, he ran for the planter, grabbed it at either edge and lifted. It was heavier than it looked. Although harder to lift, that should make it even more effective for his purposes.

He made it back behind the corner of the house before another shot was fired. Resting for only a second, he pulled in a deep breath and heaved the planter through the patio door's window.

Glass shattered and scattered in tiny, rounded pebbles over the patio. The scream of the smoke alarms burst out along with a haze of smoke. He grabbed the sheer curtain stretched tight over the opening and gave a yank. The light fabric ripped from its rod and flapped to the ground.

Gray scooped in one last clean breath and stepped through the opening, angling his body to slide through.

Once inside, he lowered himself to hands and knees. Smoke rose, and if he had any hopes of finding breathable air, he needed to stay as close to the floor as possible. He could only hope Natalie was doing the same.

If she was still alive.

He pushed the possibility of anything else from his mind. He wasn't even certain she was still in the house. But he needed to focus on searching every inch. He'd meant what he promised Thad. If Natalie was here, he'd find her.

Or he'd die trying.

He crawled through the dinette. Smoke burned his eyes and caused tears to run down his cheeks. He could still see, but he wasn't sure how long that would last. He needed to hurry.

He swept the kitchen with his gaze then moved on to the living area. No sign of Natalie there, either. He made for the hall leading to the other rooms. As he moved into the narrow space, the fumes grew thicker. He blinked back their sting and kept moving.

The lack of windows in the hallway combined with the thicker smoke made seeing anything difficult, if not impossible. He couldn't keep his eyes open. Even when he did, the area was so dim and gray, he had a hard time making out his hand when he held it in front of his face.

He reached out his left hand and dragged his fingertips along the wall to keep his bearings. With each scoot forward, he swung his right leg out to scrape across the floor, feeling for Natalie where he could no longer see. He coughed with every other breath, the fumes hot and foul.

He heard the sound of flame up ahead, snapping and crackling in a low background roar. If Natalie was in this part of the house, he had to find her now. Most people who died in a fire perished from the smoke. He had to hurry.

Sweat trickled down his back and neck. He shucked his jacket then kept moving. The hall had never seemed long, but navigating it blind while crawling in this awkward way seemed to take forever. The door to the studio had to be here somewhere.

Light glowed from his right, slightly orange in the gray haze. The studio. Natalie's paintings. Judging from the broken pane he'd noticed outside, whoever had done this likely tossed a Molotov cocktail through the window as well as the front door, aiming to burn the paintings and trap Natalie inside.

He swept his right foot wide, dragging his toe along the baseboard. The wall gave way to the indentation of the studio's doorway. His foot ran into something soft and solid.

Natalie.

He found her with his hands. He skimmed

his fingers over her face. Her body was warm, but with the heat in the hallway, he wasn't sure that meant anything. He found her throat and felt for a pulse. The beat thrummed steadily against his fingertips.

She was alive. *Thank God, she was alive.*

Now he had to get her out of there so she'd stay that way.

He rolled to his side and draped her arm over his shoulder. Grabbing her wrist, he heaved her onto his back and caught her leg with his other hand.

He could feel her cough, her diaphragm moving in a spasm. She gripped his hand.

"I'm here, babe. I've got you."

"Trying to get out." She coughed several times and muttered more words he couldn't understand, ending with "...to the bedroom."

"Okay, to the bedroom. We're going to get out of this mess."

"No, the window. No, jammed." She seemed disoriented, but he understood the gist of what she was trying to say.

Probably nailed shut the way the patio door had been. He felt for the wall, trying to recalibrate his sense of direction. "Okay. I have another way out. Leave it to me. You just hold on as tight as you can."

"You hold on, too."

"You bet I will, Nat. No matter what happens, I'll never let you go."

She clung to him as he crawled along the wall. He made it out of the hall in much less time than it had taken going in, now that he didn't have to search. His knees were sore from crawling, his head ached to high heaven and his lungs felt like glowing, red cigarette ash. He hoped the fumes of the paints weren't toxic. He had no idea how long the studio had been aflame or how that might affect Natalie.

He pushed those worries to the back of his mind and kept moving. If he didn't get them out of here, he needn't concern himself with anything else.

He made it into the living room and took a turn into the dinette. The hardwood floor made his knees ache even more. Natalie gripped his hand, still coughing. Now that they were away from the fire, he could hear the rasp of each of her breaths.

They reached the patio door. Fresh air streamed through the hole. Glass crunched under his knees. Uncomfortable, but since it was tempered, it wasn't sharp. "I'm going to stand up, Nat. Hold tight."

She squeezed his hand.

He climbed to his feet. Stepping through the hole he'd bashed in the door, he angled

Natalie to the side so they could both fit through.

Now he had to pray Thad had been able to what he'd promised.

He lowered Natalie to the patio, snug in the lee of the cottage. The shooter could have changed positions while he'd been in the burning structure. He had no way of knowing. He just hoped by keeping low, they could avoid being spotted.

Natalie doubled forward in a coughing spasm.

He stroked her hair and blinked his eyes, letting his tears cleanse away the smoke. Now that he could begin to see a little more in the light and fresh air, he noticed a rosy cast to her skin. The wind whipped around them, cooling his sweat-soaked shirt and chilling his skin, but Natalie's color didn't fade.

God, no.

He knew what that color meant, why she'd been on the floor, why she'd been disoriented. Why he had a splitting headache and nausea from the short time he'd been inside.

Carbon monoxide.

Her cells were filled with it. So filled they couldn't accept oxygen. If he didn't get her medical help, she would die.

He slipped one arm under her legs, one

under her back. "I'm going to take you to the hos—"

He felt the bullet hit before he heard the report.

The force of the impact shoved him forward onto Natalie. Cold sliced through his chest and spread through his body. He gasped for breath, but as hard as he strained, it wouldn't seem to come. "Nat?"

Footsteps crunched through the fall garden, slowly coming toward them.

Gray forced himself up, bracing himself into a sitting position with his hands. Still struggling to breathe, he looked down at the blood covering Natalie.

His blood. God, let it be his blood alone.

Pain breaking through some of the frigid cold claiming his body, he twisted to look at the shooter.

The man held his assault rifle in front of him, finger on the trigger. Brows low and mouth in a tight smile, he looked at Gray with hard eyes.

Eyes that Gray recognized. "You."

Gray should have thought of him. Maybe he should have known, but he hadn't. Whoever this guy was, he wanted to kill Natalie. He wanted to finish what he'd intended ever since that night he'd followed her from the coffee shop.

He raised the rifle to his shoulder. "Get out of the way," he said.

Gray threw his body over Natalie's. The bullet would go through both of them. He couldn't stop it. But he couldn't just give up. He had to do anything, everything, *something* to save her life.

A shot exploded in his ears.

Chapter Eighteen

Gray never thought he'd wake up. But when he opened his eyes, Thad was pulling him up from Natalie and pushing his jacket against the wound in his chest. "Where is he?"

Thad glanced at something on the ground, something Gray couldn't see. "Dead."

Gray grabbed the jacket from Thad and propped himself into a hunched forward sitting position. The past few moments shuffled through his mind. The rifle pointing at Natalie. Covering her with his body. The shot ringing in his ears. "You were the one who fired?"

Thad nodded. He knelt down beside Natalie.

Sirens screamed from somewhere in the distance. "You found a way to call out?"

"Must have been the neighbors. Is Natalie…"

"The blood is mine. But she's in rough shape. Carbon monoxide."

Thad nodded at Gray's chest. "Looks like you're in rough shape, too."

He glanced down at himself. Blood already soaked Thad's jacket. Breathing was becoming difficult. He felt dizzy. Weak. "Only because you kicked the hell out of me earlier."

Thad gave a strained laugh.

Gray tried to laugh along, but it ended up in a series of choking coughs that felt like they were ripping his body apart.

When the coughs subsided, he glanced back at Thad. "The shooter. I recognized him."

"Who was he?"

"Name is Wade. All I know. Could be fake." He shook his head, wishing he'd realized the Romeo wannabe was really a dangerous threat from the first.

"Why was he trying to kill Natalie?"

"I have no clue."

Police cars streamed into the driveway, an ambulance behind.

Gray leaned heavily forward on his hands and struggled for breath. Then everything went black.

When Natalie woke in the hospital, her throat was more sore than it had ever been in her life, including all the times she'd had strep throat as a kid. A heart monitor beeped at her bedside. A plastic tube snaked under her nose and looped behind her ears. A medicinal smell hung in the air.

"Welcome back."

She looked in the direction of the voice and focused on a face. A face she hadn't seen for a long time. Her heart gave a little hop. "Thad," she whispered in a croaking voice.

He smiled. His blue eyes twinkled. "Am I glad to see you. You just missed Aunt Angela."

"You're home." She probably sounded stupid, stating the obvious like that. But she could hardly believe it. It was so good to see him.

"I have been back in St. Louis for a few days now."

"A few days?" She didn't understand.

"You're in the ICU. You've been here for three days, recovering from carbon monoxide poisoning. You were on a respirator, so they kept you knocked out."

She shook her head. She didn't remember how she'd gotten here. She had no idea she'd been asleep that long.

Thad narrowed his eyes on her. "How much do you remember?"

She searched the images in her mind, the

feelings. "I remember Ash and Rachel's wedding. The shooting. And the night after..." She pressed her lips together, keeping the events of that night to herself. But as soon as she recalled making love with Gray, the rest came back, too. Gray leaving her. And Chet, lying motionless in the garden. "My bodyguard, is he okay?"

"You mean Gray?"

She shook her head. "Gray? Was Gray hurt?"

Thad nodded. Holding her hand carefully so as not to disturb the IV needle in her hand, he propped one hip on the edge of her bed. "You remember the fire?"

She nodded.

"The cottage. The man who was trying to kill you started it on fire."

Shock vibrated through her. She remembered bits. The smell of smoke. The choking panic. The darkness and confusion.

"The firefighters put it out. But there was a lot of smoke damage. Gray Scott, he was the one who rescued you. He was shot in the chest."

Her breath hitched.

"It's okay," Thad said. "He's going to be all right."

She let out a shuddering breath. "And Chet?"

"He was killed. He was dead before Gray or I got there. I'm sorry."

She lay still for a long time, her brother holding her hand, gently rubbing her fingers. So much had happened she wasn't sure if she could ever get it all straight in her head. "And the man who shot Gray and Chet?"

He was quiet for a long while. Finally he said, "I took him out."

"You? How?"

Thad explained what happened, blow by blow. When he was finished, Natalie was able to connect some pieces in her mind, although most parts were still foggy. But out of all the traumatic things that had taken place, the hardest thing for her to believe was that the normal-looking guy with bad shoes was the person who'd been trying to kill her all along.

Still, she couldn't ignore it. Judging from all Thad told her, the evidence was conclusive. His fingerprints matched the ones Ash had lifted from inside the cottage after her paintings had been shredded. The oversize powder-blue sweatshirt worn by the person who'd pushed her into traffic was recovered from his apartment. And the rifle he'd used to shoot Chet and Gray matched the slugs found in Gray's apartment and outside the wedding chapel.

Natalie's head whirled. It seemed like it should all add up. It seemed like it should make sense. But try as she might, she couldn't grasp any of it. "Who *is* this Wade guy? Why would he want to kill me?"

"We don't know that yet. But believe me, all of us are working on it. Ash even postponed his honeymoon."

She knew Thad, Ash and Devin wouldn't rest until they found out the truth. She would help, too, if she could, as soon as she was well enough. "You said Gray was shot, but he's okay." Just saying the words, just thinking about Gray being hurt, made her start to tremble.

Thad nodded. "He's going to be fine. I just popped in to see him about an hour ago. He's right here in the hospital. They moved him out of ICU a couple of days ago, so I guess you could say, he's doing better than you are. When you get strong enough, I'll take you to see him."

Shivers spread over her skin. "No, that's okay."

Thad's eyebrows arched toward his closely cropped dark brown hair. "He saved your life. In fact, when Wade was about to shoot you, Gray threw himself over you. As if he thought he could shield you from the bullet."

Tears filled her eyes. The hospital whites and beiges swam in front of her, mixing until she could see nothing but a bland wash.

"You care for him, don't you?"

She didn't say anything. She couldn't.

"You love him."

A rumble of voices sounded in the hall outside. Natalie wiped her eyes just as the curtain whooshed back and Devin and Ash stepped into her ICU cubicle.

After a flurry of exclamations about her being awake and a bunch of gentle hugs, Devin focused on Thad. "Natalie loves who?" he asked.

Thad looked up at their oldest brother. "Gray Scott."

Devin frowned.

Natalie shook her head. "I don't want to talk about this."

Natalie glowered at her traitorous brother. Of course, she never could have expected Thad would stay silent on the matter of her love life, or lack thereof. All three of her brothers tended to gang up when it came to protecting her.

"Maybe we should drag him in here," said Ash. "Make him do right by our little sister."

Devin nodded. "Got any handcuffs on you?"

"Stop it, guys." Natalie had meant to throw the words at them in a joking fashion. Instead they came out on a wave of tears.

All three of her brothers stared at her with expressions of horror on their faces.

Devin hovered over her first. "I'm sorry, Natalie. Don't cry. We didn't mean to joke. You know I wasn't happy with Scott taking advantage of you in the first place. But if you love him, he should damn well be here for you. And we'll make sure he is. Better yet, we'll make sure that when he comes to visit you, he brings a diamond ring with him."

Ash nodded, joined by Thad.

Natalie closed her eyes. She knew they loved her. She knew they meant well. But they didn't understand. "Don't you dare say one word to Gray. Understand?"

She looked at her brothers in turn, waiting for each to nod, before she went on. "I don't want a man to ask me to marry him because my big brothers bully him into doing it."

She wiped her eyes with the hand not hooked up to the IV. "I'll admit it. Most of my life, I've dreamed of getting married, of having my own family, of having a man who would never leave me. But I can see how misguided that is now. How it led to me grabbing for whatever male attention I could get, just so I could get a ring, just so I wouldn't be alone."

Her throat closed. She held up a hand to keep her brothers from interrupting until she could regain her composure. "I used to want to get married for marriage's sake, I guess. Because I thought it would give me something I didn't have. But my priorities have changed. I don't want that anymore."

Thad squeezed her hand and gave her an understanding smile. "We only want the best for you, Natalie. You know that."

Her other two brothers nodded their agreement.

"I know. And the best for me is a man who wants to be with me. A man whom I don't have to worry will leave me, because he loves me so much, he doesn't want to be anywhere else." The short time she'd known Gray had taught her that. And after all she'd felt with him—even though it hadn't lasted— she wasn't going to settle for anything less from here on out. "If he loves me enough, he'll come to me. If he doesn't, he's not the one."

All her brothers beamed at her. Devin was the first to speak. "I'm so glad to hear you say that, Natalie. You deserve the best. And I hope you really do believe it, because the three of us, we always have."

GRAY'S CHEST HURT LIKE hell as he slowly climbed from his car and hobbled up to the three-story gray stone mansion, and he doubted the fact that his heart was beating faster than a damn rabbit's helped the issue. He had no idea if Natalie would agree to see him. He wouldn't blame her if she didn't. But whatever the case, he wasn't leaving until he'd had his chance to speak.

He pushed the button to the right of the grand front door. Chimes echoed through the entry hall. Before long, footsteps clicked on the marble floor inside. The door opened and Natalie's uncle Craig peered out.

"Hello, Mr. Kendall. I'm here to see Natalie." He felt as nervous as a teenager, even though his body ached like an old man's.

Craig Kendall frowned. At first, Gray thought the man would brush him off, order him to get lost. Instead, he pulled the door wide and let Gray step inside.

"Wait here," he said, and walked from the foyer.

Gray fumbled with the box in his pocket. He let his gaze skim up the split staircase, one branch leading to the east wing, one to the west. It had been almost two weeks since he and Natalie had gone off in their opposite directions. At first he had no hope of them ever coming back together. Then he knew he had to do something, that he could never go on if he didn't try to fix what he'd broken.

Now he was here to give it his all.

Natalie stepped into the foyer. Dressed in jeans and a sweatshirt, she had her hair pulled into a ponytail. She eyed him, a little wary, but boldly met him in the center of the wide marble floor. "It's good to see you."

He hoped she really meant that. "You look good. How are you feeling?"

"Pretty good. More like myself every day. And you?" She glanced down at his chest. She couldn't see the bandages still wrapping his torso, but judging by the look on her face, she had picked up the fact that he was still less than one hundred percent.

"I'm okay. Healing."

She nodded.

He hated the fact that they were so stiff with one another, so awkward. He wanted the teasing flirtiness back, a tone that had always bloomed so naturally between them. "I miss you."

She pressed her lips together and nodded, as if she was unable to speak.

He wanted to pull her into his arms, to kiss her until all the hurts between them went away. But he realized she wasn't ready for that. He didn't know if she'd be ready for him to touch her ever again. "I'm so sorry for leaving you that day."

She nodded again.

His chest ached, but not from the gunshot wound. That pain would fade in the weeks and months ahead. He had no idea if the wounds between them could ever heal. All he knew was that he needed to tell her everything that was in his heart. That was all he could do. "I realize I screwed up. In trying to take responsibility for everything, I didn't own the one thing I needed to. The one thing that is most important. I love you, Natalie."

A slip of a whimper sounded deep in her throat.

"Duty and responsibility and doing the right thing—it doesn't mean anything to me without you in my life. I can't go through a second of the day without thinking of you. I can't sleep at night without dreaming of all the ways I screwed up. I don't know if you can forgive me or even if you want to, but I love you, Natalie Kendall. And I can't go one more day without telling you that."

She stepped toward him. "I love you, too, Gray."

His breath caught in his throat. Her words were all he wanted, all he needed.

He took her in his arms and brought his lips down to hers. Her kiss was the sweetest thing he'd ever tasted. And when he looked back into her eyes, his own vision was misty with tears. "In the fire, I promised I'd never leave you, that I'd never let you go. I meant it, Natalie. I realize I can't control the world. That I can't take care of everyone. That it isn't even my duty to try. But I want to take care of you, if you'll have me."

She nodded. A little smile touched her lips. "How about if we try taking care of each other?"

No wonder he loved her so. "Yes. That sounds right. We take care of each other for the rest of our lives."

He grabbed a deep breath and lowered himself to one knee. His bad knee was stiff and both were still bruised, but he didn't care. He'd gone through worse in combat;

the least he could do was sacrifice a little comfort for love.

He reached into his pocket and pulled out the velvet box. Opening it, he held it up in one hand for Natalie to see, clutching her hand in the other. "Natalie Kendall, will you marry me?"

She pressed her lips together and frowned down at him. "Did my brothers put you up to this?"

He tilted his head. Not exactly the response he'd expected. "Your brothers? Are you kidding?"

A laugh bubbled from her lips.

He still didn't get it. Maybe she was making a joke. "They'd probably be more eager to break my kneecaps than see me propose."

She knelt down beside him on the cold marble floor. Tears filled her eyes, making her green irises sparkle like they were made of emeralds. "Yes, Gray. I'll marry you."

He took her face in his hands and kissed her lips, her cheeks, her cute little nose. Her tears tasted salty on his tongue. Her skin smelled like heaven.

They slid down until they were both sitting

on the floor in the big, formal foyer, holding each other. And Gray knew from that moment on, he would never, ever let her go.

Epilogue

Thanksgiving at the Kendall mansion had always been something spectacular. Turkey and stuffing, cranberries and pumpkin pie. The works. They ate like gluttons, then watched the St. Louis Rams take on the Dallas Cowboys. Then after the game, they ate some more.

Natalie had been so proud to have Gray sitting at the long, festive table beside her. He held her hand under the tablecloth, twirling her ring around and around her finger. And that night, even though neither of them was yet in the best health, he stayed with her in her newly refurbished cottage.

The next day was set aside for one of Natalie's favorite holiday treats. Trimming the tree. After Thad and Ash cut a gorgeous fir, the whole family gathered in the mansion's large living room.

Aunt Angela and Jolie opened boxes of

ornaments while Devin and Uncle Craig strung the lights. Rachel passed out plates of leftover wedding cake to anyone who would have some. And the rest of them waited their turn to hang their favorite ornaments, some of which they'd had since they were children.

When they were stuffed with white almond cake with chocolate mousse filling and buttercream frosting, Gray pulled Natalie off to a quiet corner. "I know this is bad timing, but I need to talk to you about something I noticed. Something that's been bothering me for a while."

In the past, a comment like that would have sent Natalie's heart racing. She would have been certain he was going to tell her he was unhappy, announce there was nothing left for him to do but leave. But this time, she was certain none of those nightmares would play themselves out. She felt totally at ease. Totally sure of the man beside her. Concerned only that something might be causing him unease. "What is it?"

He dipped a hand into his pocket, pulled out a photograph and handed it to her.

She looked down at the picture. It was the face of the man at the coffee shop, the murderer who'd killed poor Chet and tried to kill both of them. Her heart gave a little shudder.

She glanced back up at Gray. "What about him?"

"The day of the fire, I noticed something. I kept telling myself it's not important, that it's really nothing, but I can't let it go."

"I don't understand. What?"

"Does he look familiar to you?"

She looked back at the picture. It had been taken by the police, after the man was dead. The whole idea of looking at a dead body this way was pretty creepy. The fact that the last time he'd been alive he'd tried to kill them made it even worse.

"What do you think?" Gray prompted.

"There is something that's bothered me, too." Now that Gray had brought it up, she could no longer deny the niggle at the back of her mind whenever she'd thought of the mysterious Wade. She'd been haunted by his features, too, seen his face in her dreams, and she still had no clue why. "I can't help thinking that maybe I should know him. He looks kind of familiar to me."

Gray frowned. "He looks like you."

"What?"

"Without the brown eyes. Not as pretty, obviously. Don't take this the wrong way, Natalie, but Wade, whoever he was, looks more like you than your own brothers do."

She looked back down at the picture and pressed her hands between her knees to keep them from trembling. "You really think so? What does that mean?"

"Maybe nothing." Gray slipped an arm around her and held her close. "But I think we should find out."

She didn't want to think too hard about what finding out could mean. Not until she had to. "You're thinking about a DNA test?"

"Rachel could take a swab from the inside of your cheek right now. If the crime lab is too backed up, we could take it to a private lab, have the test expedited. Maybe it will tell us who he really is. And if he's related to you, maybe that will explain why he tried to kill you."

She felt a chill work up her spine. Arm still tight around her, Gray rubbed her shoulder with his fingers.

She looked into his eyes and nodded. "I want to know the truth. And whatever it is, I know I can take it. I can handle anything with you and my family by my side."

He brought his lips to hers and gave her a gentle kiss. "And I'm never leaving."

She couldn't help but smile. "I know."

* * * * *

*Don't miss the heart-stopping conclusion
of* SITUATION: CHRISTMAS—
*DADDY BOMBSHELL,
by reader favorite Lisa Childs.
Look for it wherever
Harlequin Intrigue books are sold!*

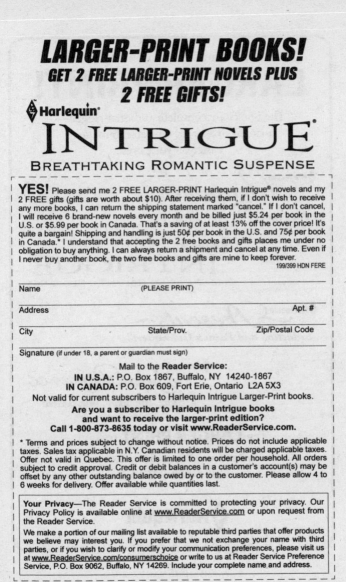

LARGER-PRINT BOOKS!
GET 2 FREE LARGER-PRINT NOVELS PLUS
2 FREE GIFTS!

⬥ Harlequin®

INTRIGUE®

BREATHTAKING ROMANTIC SUSPENSE

YES! Please send me 2 FREE LARGER-PRINT Harlequin Intrigue® novels and my 2 FREE gifts (gifts are worth about $10). After receiving them, if I don't wish to receive any more books, I can return the shipping statement marked "cancel." If I don't cancel, I will receive 6 brand-new novels every month and be billed just $5.24 per book in the U.S. or $5.99 per book in Canada. That's a saving of at least 13% off the cover price! It's quite a bargain! Shipping and handling is just 50¢ per book in the U.S. and 75¢ per book in Canada.* I understand that accepting the 2 free books and gifts places me under no obligation to buy anything. I can always return a shipment and cancel at any time. Even if I never buy another book, the two free books and gifts are mine to keep forever.

199/399 HDN FERE

Name _____ (PLEASE PRINT) _____

Address _____ Apt. # _____

City _____ State/Prov. _____ Zip/Postal Code _____

Signature (if under 18, a parent or guardian must sign) _____

Mail to the **Reader Service:**
IN U.S.A.: P.O. Box 1867, Buffalo, NY 14240-1867
IN CANADA: P.O. Box 609, Fort Erie, Ontario L2A 5X3
Not valid for current subscribers to Harlequin Intrigue Larger-Print books.

**Are you a subscriber to Harlequin Intrigue books
and want to receive the larger-print edition?
Call 1-800-873-8635 today or visit www.ReaderService.com.**

* Terms and prices subject to change without notice. Prices do not include applicable taxes. Sales tax applicable in N.Y. Canadian residents will be charged applicable taxes. Offer not valid in Quebec. This offer is limited to one order per household. All orders subject to credit approval. Credit or debit balances in a customer's account(s) may be offset by any other outstanding balance owed by or to the customer. Please allow 4 to 6 weeks for delivery. Offer available while quantities last.

Your Privacy—The Reader Service is committed to protecting your privacy. Our Privacy Policy is available online at www.ReaderService.com or upon request from the Reader Service.

We make a portion of our mailing list available to reputable third parties that offer products we believe may interest you. If you prefer that we not exchange your name with third parties, or if you wish to clarify or modify your communication preferences, please visit us at www.ReaderService.com/consumerschoice or write to us at Reader Service Preference Service, P.O. Box 9062, Buffalo, NY 14269. Include your complete name and address.

HILP11B